"Where are you going?"

She scrambled after him, only to trip halfway down the stairs. One moment she was stepping on solid ground, and the next her feet flailed into emptiness. Before she could scream, strong arms grasped her beneath her legs and back.

"I've got you," Liam said.

She buried her head against his broad chest; the crisp linen of his dress shirt smelled detergent clean and Harper relaxed against him until the wild beating of her heart mellowed.

Liam picked up several tiny metal objects from the steps. "What's this?"

It couldn't be—yet she couldn't deny the solid proof in front of her. "Jacks."

"Like, in the kid's game?"

She retrieved the jack from his hand and closed her fist around the six-pointed metallic piece, with enough pressure that the sharp nubs indented her flesh. This child's game piece was real—nothing ghostly about its solid substance.

"Yes," she whispered. "Presley and I used to play jacks together all the time."

"That doesn't explain how they got here."

UNMASKING THE SHADOW MAN

USA TODAY Bestselling Author

DEBBIE HERBERT

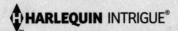

This book is dedicated to Karen Groce; thanks for being such
a great beta reader!

And, as always, to my husband, Tim; my dad, J. W. Gainey;
and my sons, Byron and Jacob.

ISBN-13: 978-1-335-60468-2

Unmasking the Shadow Man

Recycling programs
for this product may
not exist in your area.

Copyright © 2019 by Debbie Herbert

Printed in U.S.A.

www.Harlequin.com

USA TODAY bestselling author **Debbie Herbert** writes paranormal romance novels reflecting her belief that love, like magic, casts its own spell of enchantment. She's always been fascinated by magic, romance and gothic stories. Married and living in Alabama, she roots for the Crimson Tide football team. Her eldest son, like many of her characters, has autism. Her youngest son is in the US Army. A past Maggie Award finalist in both young adult and paranormal romance, she's a member of the Georgia Romance Writers of America.

Visit the Author Profile page at Harlequin.com.

CAST OF CHARACTERS

Harper Catlett—Haunted by the strange circumstances of her sister's death, Harper can never forget awakening as a child and finding her sister motionless at the foot of the stairs. She momentarily glimpsed what appeared to be a monster hovering over the body. Nobody takes her story seriously, and when strange things reoccur decades later, only one man is willing to help her solve the mystery of her past.

Liam Andrews—Posing as a new cop, Liam is actually an undercover FBI agent investigating a string of unsolved murders. He's been ordered to look into possible police incompetence, negligence or even the possibility that one of the local officers might be a serial killer. Secretly, he has his own agenda in accepting this assignment.

Bryce Fairfax—Baysville's current police chief and a close friend of Harper's murdered sister.

Theodore—Liam's missing uncle, who left the family as a teenager to ride the railroads and travel the country. He was never heard from again.

The Shadow Man—A figure of legend, described as a filthy, emaciated creature that vanishes the instant he's spotted. When items go missing—a jacket, a pecan pie—locals laughingly blame the Shadow Man. Adults dismiss this story.

Chapter One

The scratching began again. *Skreek.* A heartbeat of silence. *Skreek. Skreek.*

She could sleep through the blare of traffic in Atlanta, but this teeny noise in her mom's old house in rural Virginia had roused her from deep sleep in a mere nanosecond.

It was the sound of her nightmares. The ominous scratching that had preceded the worst moment of her life and hounded Harper to this day. It was inexorably tied to the image of her sister Presley's body lying on the kitchen floor as smoke swirled and fire licked the darkness. Harper sat up in bed and waited for the scratching to resume. But this time, the only noise was a faint swish of something soft brushing against a wall.

Probably just a mouse scampering behind the old Sheetrock, or so she hoped. Disgusting as that was, she'd welcome the prospect of mice infiltration over creepier alternatives. As a child, she'd wondered if the house was haunted by a ghost—or an even scarier type of supernatural horror.

Harper pictured the wraithlike, filthy creature she'd glimpsed the night Presley died. The thing—she wasn't sure if it was a person or some remnant from a dream—had loomed over her sister's lifeless body. She'd screamed, and the pale figure had vanished into the shadows. Never to be seen again.

Nobody had believed her. There'd been no signs of forced entry, and a search of the old Victorian had revealed nothing unusual. Presley's death had been ruled accidental.

But even now, the skin at the nape of her neck prickled at the memory.

This wouldn't do. After all, she'd returned to Baysville in order to settle her mom's estate and make peace with her own disturbing past. Time to discover what was real and what was imaginary. Over the years, she'd pushed that night's events to the back of her mind.

Of course, she wasn't always successful. At unexpected moments, a vivid image of pale skin draped on a frail, gaunt figure would crystallize from the hazy memories of the night Presley died.

Sleep was no longer possible, so Harper climbed out of bed and turned on the bedside lamp. The light reassuringly spotlighted the familiar and mercifully vacant room. All was in order. The peach-colored walls cast a comforting warm glow. Her white French provincial bed and dresser were old but classic and had served her since childhood. She could have taken the larger master bedroom across the hall, but it still felt like Mom's room. Probably always would, no matter how many years passed after her death.

Harper donned her comfy, though tattered, pink robe and opened the bedroom door, flipping on the hall lights. The recently polished oak floors gleamed golden and reflected the bright sheen of her red hair. She gripped the iron railing of the staircase, surveyed the stairs, and then her eyes darted involuntarily to the kitchen. After all these years, she still checked to make sure no flames or smoke billowed from the room. Grimly, Harper made her way down the steps. Would she ever descend them without remembering that night?

At the bottom of the stairs, she stopped abruptly. Heat spread from her bare feet and then up her spine, tingling like an electrical shock. Someone was here. Watching. Swiftly, she turned and surveyed the empty staircase behind her. Nothing was there except for the same old portraits that lined the stairwell wall. Generations of grim Catletts stared back at her, as if in silent rebuke of her foolishness.

Skreek.

The scratching started up again. And had she heard an echo of a footfall? Harper's ears strained, but she detected nothing else. The old house had gone eerily quiet.

Stop creeping yourself out. Nothing's here but you and the rodents.

Harper strode to the den, flipping on every light switch along the way. She turned on the TV, and the reassuring voice of a morning news show filled the house's quiet void. Then she marched to the kitchen and started coffee. Familiar sounds and smells eased the niggling worry in her gut.

See? You did it. Spent another entire night by yourself here. A couple more weeks, and you won't think anything of it. Easy peasy. Onward and upward until she'd satisfied every speck of uncertainty about what had happened that night.

In the meantime... "Exterminators," she said aloud, with a determined nod. Coffee mug in hand, Harper sat at the kitchen table and fired up her laptop. This wouldn't be just any old routine extermination. No, she was booking the full Monty—the entire house wrapped in a toxic bubble by men dressed in hazmat suits. She pulled up a list of local companies and dutifully scribbled down a couple of numbers to call when their businesses opened this morning.

Taking that action, however small, made her feel more in control. One step at a time, as her mom would say. And if anyone had reason to believe in that mantra, it was Ruth Catlett. She'd buried a husband and a child, yet every day she'd risen before dawn to work at a local diner one block down the road. And if her spirits had never quite recovered from Presley's death, she managed to put on her game face in public.

And now there was one. Harper was the last of her family. Oh, sure, there were a couple of aunts and uncles and cousins scattered about Baysville, but it wasn't the same.

Harper sighed and sipped her coffee as she

stepped onto the front porch. Streaks of purple and orange illuminated the sky and were reflected in the Pagan River's rippling water. Many of the quaint shops lining the riverfront had already turned on their lights. Baysville was awakening to a new day. She'd forgotten how beautiful her hometown was. The Tidewater region of Virginia was steeped in history and picturesque in a way that a big city like Atlanta could never match. She sat in the glider for several minutes, enjoying the slower pace. No clients to meet, no ringing phones or assistants to send on errands. She'd been much too busy this past year with her interior decorating business. In some ways, it'd been therapeutic after her breakup with Doug, but she was over that disappointment. Any man that fickle and gun-shy over commitment wasn't worth the heartbreak.

The streets gradually began to fill. Slow pace or not, it was time to go in and get dressed before someone she knew spotted her in the grungy but comfy robe that was the epitome of ugly.

Inside, Harper strolled to the kitchen table and picked up the exterminators' phone numbers. There were four new emails in her inbox. She supposed she'd better check them in case of pressing business in Atlanta. Sitting down, Harper opened her email, and her eyes were immediately drawn to one subject line that blared at her in all caps:

GET OUT OF THE HOUSE

With trembling fingers, she opened the email. No message in the body of the email, only the ominous warning from a sender: loser@life.

HARPER WALKED BY the front door of the Baysville Police Department three times before resolutely squaring her shoulders and marching in. Behind the charming brick facade of the station, the interior was utilitarian and stark. The designer in her was aghast at the yellowed linoleum floors, cheap metal chairs and institutional-green walls of the lobby, but taxpayers were paying for a service, not a pleasing office aesthetic.

At the counter, a bored woman handed her a clipboard. "Write down your name and reason for coming."

Dutifully, Harper printed her name, then paused. Reason for coming? They were going to laugh her out of the station if she wrote "disturbing email." This had been a terrible idea. Growing up, other kids had merely looked at her strangely if she mentioned the thing she'd seen that night. Worse, she hated that look of pity as they scooted away from her. As though she was a sort of magnet for disaster. It had been high school before her friendships had returned to normal, and that was due in large part to making the cheerleading squad and becoming friends with the popular Kimber Collins. Harper had learned to fit in with her peer group, keep her mouth shut and act as if all was well in her world.

"Never mind," she told the city employee, handing back the clipboard.

She blinked at her behind thick glasses. Before the woman could ask questions, Harper flashed a fake smile and turned away.

"Excuse me, miss, are you sure about this?" the woman called out.

The few others slouched in the lobby waiting area looked up from their cell phones. Harper ignored them, too, as she waved a hand, the phony smile still in place. She looked and felt like an utter fool. All she wanted was a quick exit and...

Oomph. She crashed into a solid object and began tumbling backward. Hands gripped her forearm.

"Whoa, there. You okay?"

Dark, amused eyes flashed before her face. Bryce Fairfax.

Harper's face and neck heated. "Fine," she mumbled. Maybe if she hurried, he wouldn't recognize her. She tried to pull away, but he held fast.

"Harper Catlett, Presley's little sister," he said, flashing his infamous grin that had had all the girls swooning in high school, including Presley. Truth be told, Harper had secretly crushed on him, too, although he was a good nine years older than her.

His smile faded. "Sorry to hear about your mom. I imagine you've been busy with her estate and settling loose ends."

"Yes, thanks."

His grip loosened but still remained. "What brings

you to my station? Is there anything I can help you with?"

"Well, no. It's not important."

Bryce tugged at her arm and guided her back into the station. She fell into step beside him, wishing like hell that she'd never come.

"I'd do any favor for Presley's little sister. Did you know that in high school, she used to tutor me in algebra? If it wasn't for her, I might have failed that class. As it was, I managed to slip by with a D-minus."

His self-deprecating laugh eased some of her tension. Bryce was as charming as ever. He had a knack for drawing people to him, especially women. He'd kept his athletic physique, and the crinkles at the corners of his eyes and forehead only made him look more interesting.

"Yes, I knew about the tutoring. Presley was so smart. Wish she'd been around when I struggled with math classes."

Bryce shot her a sympathetic nod. "Such a tragic accident."

"If it was an accident…" Harper clamped her mouth shut. No sense reminding anyone about her so-called mystery monster.

His brows rose, but he didn't respond as they passed through the lobby and into the bowels of the station. From here, the slamming of iron doors and loud voices emanated from the county jail connected to the back of the building. It was disquieting. Any moment, she expected an escaped convict to pop out of nowhere, looking for a hostage.

At the end of a narrow hallway, she followed Bryce into his private office. She'd expected more from the police chief's office, although she shouldn't have been surprised, given the rest of the station's decor.

Bryce slid behind a massive desk constructed of dark-stained plywood. A simple nameplate on his desk displayed his name and title. "About what you said back there—" he clasped his hands on the desk and leaned forward slightly, all business "—are you saying that you believe Presley's death wasn't accidental?"

"Not at all. I mean, I was only a child when it happened. What do I know?"

His dark eyes pierced her, as if trying to read her mind. "I remember the rumors. You claimed to have seen something—or someone—by Presley's body right after she fell."

She swallowed hard. "Like I said, I was a kid. One with a vivid imagination and who had awakened from a bad dream. A bad combination."

"Describe what you saw, again."

Harper shifted in her seat, uncomfortable with the request. "It sounds so silly now. I thought I saw a stick-thin person wearing filthy rags and staring at me with huge eyes."

They were like the alien eyes that people drew after supposed encounters with UFO creatures, unnaturally large and black. But she didn't elaborate on the details. Even now, the memory unnerved her. Harper rubbed the goose bumps on her arms.

Another cop entered the room and shoved a piece of paper across the desk to Bryce. The man was tall and exuded authority in the firm set of his shoulders. He shot her a curious glance, his gray eyes quickly assessing her. She had the feeling he'd overheard some of the conversation. Probably pegged her as a wacko. A nuisance taking up the boss's time.

Bryce nodded at the cop. "I'll call him back in a few minutes. Stay a moment while I finish up here. I have some questions for you on this matter. Harper, this is Officer Andrews."

"Hello," she said politely.

"Harper Catlett was born and raised here in Baysville," Bryce told Andrews.

The chief turned his gaze back to her. "I can assure you the case was thoroughly investigated by this office and the fire department. No signs of forced entry, no evidence of foul play."

Great. Now she'd insulted him. "I'm certain everyone here did an excellent job," Harper hastened to agree. "I'll never forget your father was the first firefighter to respond at the scene."

"Must have been tough on you and your mom. And now she's passed away, too. Lots of bad memories here for you in Baysville. I imagine you're itching to sell the old house and get back to Atlanta."

"You know I live in Atlanta now?"

Bryce gave an easy chuckle. "You forget how

news travels in a small town. Kimber mentioned it after your mom's funeral."

"Oh. Of course." She and Kimber had kept in close touch over the years.

"Sorry I missed the funeral—I had to testify in a case south of here. I did make it late to visitation one night, though. Fifty-two years old. That's way too young to die."

Just like with her father, death had crept up sudden and silent—in the form of a heart attack. Harper would always wonder if mourning over Presley's death had been a contributing factor in her mom's early demise.

"So what brings you here today?" Bryce asked, cutting through her reverie.

"Right." She removed her cell phone from her purse and punched in the password, conscious of two sets of eyes on her. "It may seem like nothing now, but I was a little concerned this morning when this email popped up on my laptop."

"Some kind of cyberthreat?" Bryce asked. "I assure you, we take everything seriously."

Harper's brows knotted with worry. The threatening email was gone. Had she accidentally deleted it? Quickly, she scrolled through her email trash folder. Not there, either. "I, um, it seems to have disappeared," she explained reluctantly.

"That's too bad," Bryce said smoothly. "What did it say?"

"To get out of the house."

Silence greeted her words.

"Anything else?" Bryce asked.

"No. That's it, except for some strange noises in the house. Probably mice," she admitted sheepishly. "In the light of day, in front of two cops, all this doesn't sound so bad." Harper rose. "I've wasted enough of your time. Good to see you again, Bryce. Nice to meet you, Officer Andrews."

Bryce also rose. "Come back anytime. Let us know if it happens again."

His words were kind, but she felt as though he was impatient to return to work. With a quick nod and smile, she hurried to the door, glad to make an escape.

Halfway down the hallway, she turned at the sound of approaching footsteps. Officer Andrews bore down on her. "Would you like to file an official report?" he asked.

"No. Forget it. I'm sure it's nothing."

"I wouldn't say that."

She blinked at his earnest kindness.

"Especially since you believe a family member may have been murdered in that house."

He had overheard her conversation with Bryce. "I didn't exactly say that," she protested.

"Not in so many words. I don't know if Chief Fairfax mentioned it, but there's been a long string of unsolved murders in Baysville. Would it make you feel safer if an officer searched your house sometime this afternoon or evening?"

Harper hesitated. *Yes,* she wanted to scream. On the other hand, what would people say if they observed an officer in her home? The hell with appearances, she decided. She was only going to be here a short while. Might as well be able to get a sound sleep in the evenings.

"Yes, that would be great, actually. Thank you." She withdrew a pen and paper from her purse and wrote down her address and phone number. "Whoever you send, just tell them it's the last house on the left at the end of King Street."

"Got it," he said, tucking the paper in his uniform shirt pocket. "I'll have no trouble finding your place."

Was his kindness merely a scam to put a move on her? She rejected the suspicion immediately. Doug had really done a number on her mind for her to be so suspicious of a local cop doing a favor.

Harper made a quick exit, pausing at the lobby entrance. She turned around and caught both Bryce and Officer Andrews standing in the hallway, regarding her soberly.

A string of unsolved murders, Officer Andrews had said. They weren't dismissive of this threat at all. Harper didn't know whether to be relieved or worried about their concern for her safety.

Chapter Two

Harper leaned against the pillows on her mom's headboard and wearily brushed a hand through her tousled hair. Six cardboard boxes lay scattered on the floor, filled to brimming with her mother's old clothes. On the bed, she'd kept out a few things she couldn't bear to part with—a couple of Mom's old silk scarves, the flannel night robe she'd worn for decades and several sweaters that were still stylish. The rest would be donated to charity. The sooner everything was packed up, the sooner she could hold an estate sale for the furniture. Whatever didn't sell would also be given away.

Coffee was in order. Tonight, she wanted to finish the master bedroom and then move on to either the basement or attic in the morning. Harper kicked aside boxes and headed to the kitchen.

Twilight cast its dusky hue along the riverfront. Today had gone by much too quickly. There was so much to do before she returned to Atlanta and her normal routine. Without Doug. It wasn't so much that she missed him, it was being alone yet again. And now, with Mom's passing, the thought of Thanksgiving and Christmas on her own was depressing. Maybe she should book a tropical cruise and pretend the holidays weren't even taking place. The idea lifted her spirits. Her business was successful, so why not have a little fun after this sad year?

Humming, Harper measured water into the coffeepot. Might as well fill it to the brim—Officer Andrews had called earlier, saying he'd stop by after work. Didn't all cops love coffee and doughnuts? Tonight, cheesecake would have to do. Speaking of which, a tiny slice now would be a reward after all her hard work cleaning and packing. She got the dessert out of the fridge, then frowned at the dwindling size of the cheesecake. Had she really eaten that much of it in the past two days? Evidently, she had.

She limited herself to only a couple bites, eaten over the kitchen sink. A neighbor across the street, Mrs. Henley, walked down the driveway to collect her mail, which reminded Harper to check hers as well. Outside, the air was a bit chilly for October. Harper hugged her arms as she sprinted for the mailbox. She waved at Mrs. Henley, an old friend of her mom's, and then withdrew a handful of envelopes.

An icy finger of fear trickled down the nape of her neck. Someone was watching her. She lifted her head and caught a faint swish of the lace curtain hanging in her attic window. Harper drew a deep breath. Inhale, hold for four counts, and then a long exhale—just as her yoga teacher advised for easing stress. *Nobody's there.* The house had been locked up tight ever since Mom died. A couple more therapeutic breaths and she dismissed the silly feeling of being watched. The prank email this morning had her jumpy, that was all.

Quickly, she flipped through the envelopes. Mostly junk, but a couple of utility bills were due. *Call and cancel utilities for next month*—Harper added the chore to her mental checklist. By then, the house would be on the market, and…

A flash of something large came toward her at breakneck speed. A whisper of tires on asphalt, the faint scent of car exhaust—Harper's head snapped up in alarm. A black pickup truck barreled down on the wrong side of the road and aimed straight at her, its headlights blinding. Paralyzing fear kept her rooted to the spot for a couple seconds.

Get back. Her body caught up to her brain's screaming message. Harper lunged off the curb and rolled onto the sidewalk. The truck crashed into her mailbox, and then its engine revved, increasing speed. Gaping at the truck's fading taillights, she lay on one elbow and watched as it sped around King Street's sharp curve, disappearing into the night as quickly as it had arrived.

"Harper! Harper, are you all right?"

Mrs. Henley's voice seemed to come from a great distance. Harper tried to catch her breath, to let her neighbor know that she was okay, but damned if the words wouldn't form past her numbed lips.

Pain radiated from the palms of both her hands

and her right hip. Blood formed beneath the ripped knees of her jeans. She raised her hands to eye level and stared blankly at the deep abrasions marking the tender skin.

"Oh my God, Harper. Tell me you're okay." Mrs. Henley knelt beside her and wrapped an arm around her shoulders. "The nerve of some drivers! He could have killed you with his recklessness."

The reality that she'd been seconds away from possible death or disfigurement finally sank in, and Harper trembled uncontrollably. Reckless? It had seemed deliberate.

She sucked in deep breaths of the crisp air and managed a wan smile. "I'm okay, thanks."

"Let me help you up."

"No. Wait a minute." She needed to collect her wits.

"Of course." Mrs. Henley nervously scanned her prone body. "Where all are you hurt?"

Good question. "I—I think just my knees and hands and hip." She drew a deep breath and sat up. "Okay, I think I'm ready to stand now."

Mrs. Henley placed her hands under Harper's right forearm. "I'll help."

She surveyed her neighbor's somewhat frail body. "That's okay. I've got this."

The sound of a racing motor set her heart skittering. Had the truck returned to finish her off? Harper twisted around. A Baysville Police Department sedan screeched to an abrupt halt by her fallen mailbox. Officer Andrews was halfway out of the vehicle before the motor turned off.

"What happened? Are you injured?" he called, running toward them.

He was beside her, his brow furrowed with concern, assessing the situation. Harper had the oddest sensation of falling into the warmth of those gray eyes. She wanted nothing more than to lean into the broad expanse of his chest and shoulders—to draw momentary comfort from his strength and kindness.

"Some fool driver nearly ran her over," Mrs. Henley jumped in to explain. "He nearly gave me a heart attack! And he didn't even stop, just kept right on going."

"Did you get a plate number?"

"No. Sorry, Officer. It happened so fast."

Andrews turned back to Harper. "What about you?"

"All I can tell you is that it was a large black pickup truck."

"Catch the make and model?" he asked hopefully.

"No." Even if it hadn't been for the darkness and her shattered nerves, Harper couldn't have relayed that information. Vehicles were just vehicles, and she'd never bothered learning different manufacturers' specifications. Not that Officer Andrews needed to know all that.

"How bad are you hurt? Should I call an ambulance?"

"No, don't. I'm fine. Was just going to stand when you drove up."

Andrews held out his hand, and she took it without hesitation. He wouldn't let her fall. His grasp was strong, an anchor to momentarily lean on. She winced, though, as the raw patches on her palm pressed into the hard strength of his hand. Luckily, her legs and ankles were uninjured, and she stood on her own two feet again. She gave him a nod, and he released his hold.

"Thank God, you're okay." Mrs. Henley held up the stack of envelopes Harper had dropped as the truck came at her. "I believe I've gathered all your mail."

Harper took the envelopes and shook her head. How unimportant the mail seemed now.

"Let's go inside, and I'll fix you something to drink while I take your statement."

Andrews's deep voice washed over her scattered senses like a balm. "I wouldn't mind a cup of coffee."

"I can do that for you," Mrs. Henley chimed in.

"That's okay, ma'am. Thanks for your help."

Harper shot him a grateful look. Mrs. Henley meant well, but once she came in the house and settled down, she was likely to stay for hours, wanting to chitchat. While her neighbor was a perfectly lovely person, Harper didn't feel up to that.

Andrews guided her in the house and helped her get seated at the kitchen table.

"Let's get you cleaned up. Where are your first aid supplies?"

She pointed to the hallway on their left. "Second

door on the right. Should be alcohol and bandages below the sink. At least, there used to be, years ago."

He left momentarily, returning with an old, dusty bottle of rubbing alcohol, a washcloth and several square packages of gauze. Kneeling by her feet, he gently cleaned the abrasions on her knees and palms. At her slight, involuntary hiss as alcohol touched the wound, he bent low and blew on her skin to ease the pain.

Holy hell. The tender intimacy of the gesture bulldozed her senses with as much impact as when she'd crashed to the ground dodging the wayward truck. After he wrapped her palms with the gauze, he moved on to her knees and she gulped hard, fighting back unexpected tears. What was wrong with her? Was she so broken that a kindly ministration reduced her to a puddled mess?

He finished, cocking his head to the side as he regarded his handiwork. "Might want to pick up some antibiotic cream tomorrow. Just to be safe."

She cleared her throat, determined to keep her voice steady. "Thank you. I've made coffee, and there's some cheesecake in the fridge," she told him. "Help yourself."

She instructed him where to find cups and dishes. He set to work, and she watched. Andrews's presence filled the kitchen, and she was again struck by his aura of confidence. He wasn't handsome in the conventional sense like Bryce—his features were a little too sharp, his body more lean than overly muscled—but Harper was drawn to him nonetheless.

Bet the man was sorry now he'd offered to stop by and check her house. Seemed she was one problem after another lately.

Andrews sat across from her. "About that truck—I'll need to file a report on the incident."

"Okay. Sorry Mrs. Henley and I are no help in providing anything more specific, Officer."

"Liam."

She blinked. "Huh?"

"My name's Liam."

Liam. The lovely syllables washed over her.

"Why don't I get started on the house search while you finish your coffee?"

"Okay. Be warned, it's a bit of a mess with boxes everywhere. I'm getting ready to sell the place."

"Understood." He rose and regarded her with something that seemed like…interest. "So, you'll be here, what, a couple more weeks?"

"More or less."

He nodded. "I'll start in the basement and work my way up."

"Sure. I'll tag along with you. I'm fine now."

Her legs were still shaky, and she hoped Liam didn't notice. He followed her to the basement, and she was conscious of his large form so close to her own. A stirring of excitement whispered through her body. How pathetic was she? The man was merely paying a kindness. Harper flipped on light switches and flushed a bit as he examined the junky, damp room.

"Lots of Dad's old tools are still down here. Plus,

Mom always kept a large pantry of canned goods and stored holiday decorations in the basement, too. Got loads of work to do clearing it all out."

Liam shone a flashlight on the narrow overhead windows. "No sign of forced entry here."

And didn't she feel foolish. Going to the cops over a few scratching noises and a silly email?

"Onward and upward," she joked. He followed her upstairs, and they made their way through each room. Liam opened all the closets and checked the windows. With each passing room, her embarrassment grew. In the attic, he walked through and inspected the cramped space filled floor to ceiling with plastic bins. "More holiday decorations," she explained. "Mom went all out for every holiday— Valentine's, St. Patrick's Day, you name it, she had knickknacks to commemorate its occurrence." An unexpected pang of nostalgia for the old days hit her in the solar plexus. *Old* meaning the years before Presley died. There hadn't been much need to celebrate anything after that.

"This house is huge," he commented as they made their way back to the kitchen. "Come from a large family?"

"Nope. There were only two of us kids and Mom and Dad. My dad used to talk about quitting work at the factory and turning this place into a B&B. But once he died, Mom lost all interest in the project. Truthfully, I don't think she was ever gung-ho about the idea. She enjoyed waitressing at the diner.

And Presley and I didn't like the idea of sharing our home with a bunch of strangers, either."

"Sorry about your sister's accident."

Speaking of which… "How did you know of it? Were you outside the office when I spoke with Bryce?"

"Couldn't help but overhear," he said easily. "I don't like to barge in when he's in the middle of a conversation."

"Ah, I get you. Well, it's been seventeen years since she died, so you don't need to walk on eggshells when it comes to discussing what happened." Harper cast an involuntary look back over her shoulder. "She fell down in the kitchen and passed out. The soup she had on the stove caught fire. She died from a combination of a head wound and smoke inhalation."

"I see." His kind gaze sent waves of comfort through her body. Lots of people acted weird when you brought up tragedies and tried to immediately change the subject. To his credit, Liam did not. "That must have been awful for your family."

"Yeah. She was only sixteen."

"Were you two close?"

"As close as you can be when you're seven years apart. I looked up to her as a kid. Presley was smart. *Genius* kind of smart. Used to earn extra money tutoring students, including your boss."

She motioned to the table, and they sat down, this time side by side. She was hyperaware of his arms and shoulders so close to her own. Harper gripped her coffee mug with both hands to resist an impulse to reach out and touch Liam. "What about your family?" she ventured. "How long have you lived in Baysville?"

A contented smile washed over his face. "I have a huge family. Three brothers and two sisters. Most of them live in Arlington."

"Parents still living?"

"Yep. Both still kicking."

"You're lucky."

A heartbeat of silence fell between them, a locked gaze that lasted a second too long to be casual. Liam scooted his chair. "Time for me to get moving. You going to be okay here by yourself?"

"Yes, of course." They both rose at the same time, and Harper almost sighed. It would be ridiculous to start anything with her moving so soon, and she wasn't into one-night stands. Damn it.

"What the hell?" Liam frowned and strode toward the back window of the kitchen.

"What is it?"

"Look outside."

Dutifully, she walked over and stood beside him. An elliptical flashlight beam pierced the marshlands abutting the far side of her property. Liam hurried out onto the back porch, and Harper grabbed the flashlight she always kept on the chifforobe for emergencies. By the time she joined up with Liam, they were halfway across her yard.

"Get back," he ordered. "I'll check it out."

"Alone?"

"I'm a cop."

"Shouldn't you at least call a dispatcher before you take off to investigate potential danger?"

"It's one person with a flashlight. And I have my cell phone on me. Not to mention a sidearm. Stay inside," he added. "Until I'm sure the area's safe."

But instead she fell into step behind him. "I'd feel safer with you."

They walked away from the lights of town and into the dark silence of the marshes. Cordgrass leaves brushed against her thighs, and her sneakers sank slightly into the muck covered by black needlerush. In the distance, flowing river water lapped against the shore, and the occasional hoot of an owl punctuated the night. Moonbeams glowed silver on the tips of cypress trees and wax myrtles.

Again, the inky blackness was pierced by a flashlight beam, but it was farther away now.

"Whoever it was, they're leaving," she whispered.

Liam turned her flashlight on full beam and directed it toward whoever had been lurking. "Damn. If I thought I could trust you not to run after me, I'd give chase."

"Good thing I'm here, then."

He shot her a severe frown. "I'm going in a little closer anyway to see what he might have been up to."

"We're getting near the railroad tracks. Probably a vagrant wandering the area."

"Awful brave of him, considering the several recent murders."

"Several?" she asked in alarm.

"Over the past ten years, six have been reported. All were vagrants. You weren't aware of this?"

"I'd heard of a couple over the years, but I didn't realize there were so many. That's awful. Have they been fighting among themselves, like some sort of gang war?"

"That's one theory," he said drily.

"I take it that's not your favorite theory."

The rev of an engine sounded from far away, but no headlights appeared.

"Think that's our flashlight man—or woman?" she asked.

"If it is, he's definitely up to no good."

"Or she," Harper remarked. "I'm an equal-opportunity crime theorist."

"Fine. You go home and theorize up a storm. Can you see well enough to make it back?"

"Sure. I left the porch light on."

"Great. I'm going to investigate."

She'd said she could see the way home, but not that she'd obey. "Be careful," she answered, turning around and taking a few steps. Once Liam was out of sight, she stopped and waited. Better to be here and learn what he'd found firsthand than to sit at home waiting and wondering. And no doubt every tiny rustle in the house would set her imagination down a fearful path she was sick of traveling.

Headlights beamed from far off, appearing for an instant and then vanishing along the winding county road out of town.

Harper shivered and wished she'd thought to grab

a jacket from the porch. Liam moved quickly through the marsh, the flashlight beam set on high and shining in an arc over the wetland field. Whatever was out there, she hoped it wasn't dangerous. She wished they would return to her house and call for backup—in case of trouble.

A hoot owl screeched, and chills bristled her skin. According to legend, the night's predatory raptor had cried a message of death.

Chapter Three

There. He'd almost stepped on the prone body lying facedown in the boggy soil. Liam shone his light on the victim, automatically categorizing details—Caucasian male, approximately six feet tall, long brown hair, wearing jeans, army boots and a flannel jacket shredded in the back upper torso area. Beneath the jagged slits, blood oozed from multiple lacerations.

It fit the pattern.

As he'd told Harper, this had been going on for years. Whoever the murderer was, he was smart enough to space the crimes out. The choice of victims was calculated, too. Usually, the homeless had cut ties with their families, and no one would report them missing for years—if ever. It was entirely possible that his missing uncle Teddy had met a similarly violent end in the backwoods of some small town. Perhaps even this one. Liam shook off the speculation to focus on his duty. Before he called out a team, he wanted to take a good look at the scene for himself. He knelt and searched the ground near the body for small clues—a button, a gum wrapper, anything the killer might have left behind unnoticed.

But there was nothing incriminating to be found.

Not only was the killer smart, but he was as cowardly as he was vicious. Each victim had been attacked from behind and stabbed multiple times. Liam pulled out his cell phone, hit the dispatcher contact button and quickly explained the situation.

A limb snapped nearby. "Officer?" a deep voice called out from the darkness. "That you, Officer Andrews?"

A group of about half a dozen men approached, in various states of dishevelment and sporting long hair and beards. Liam recognized a few of their faces.

One of the men stepped forward while the others lingered in the dark. "It's Gunner, sir. We out here lookin' for our buddy—Larry."

"When did you last see him?"

"It were morning time. He gathered up our spare change and offered to go into town to buy us a few veggies for our stew tonight. Nobody seen him since."

"Does your friend have long brown hair? Dressed in a flannel jacket?"

"Yes, sir. You seen him?"

"Unfortunately, I believe I have." Liam waved him over. "Brace yourself. It's not a pretty sight."

Liam turned the flashlight on the body for a brief second. "That look like him?"

Gunner sank to his knees, gagging.

Liam gave him a moment, then asked, "Did you see anyone roaming around here minutes ago?"

"We saw a light and headed right over in the general direction."

"Larry have a beef with anyone in town that you know of?"

"No, sir. He ain't been in Baysville but a week or two."

That was often their way. Ride the rails, then jump track to stay in a town for a bit until the urge hit to travel again. It made tracking someone damn difficult. Easy to get lost in this counterculture. Years ago they were referred to as hobos, a word probably derived from poor migrant workers who traveled from town to town toting knapsacks and a hoe for working the fields.

Baysville had once been a boomtown for them. Plenty of work in the old tobacco and corn fields. During the off-season, they could sometimes find jobs in the pork-processing factories. But these days, Baysville's largest industry was tourism, and those farm and factory jobs for transients had almost dried up.

"If you don't mind, I'd like you and your friends to stick around a bit longer. Might have a few more questions for y'all after forensics arrive and we search the area."

"Yes, sir."

Gunner clearly would rather slink away than face a group of cops, but Liam figured he knew better than to take off.

Looked like he'd be here awhile as well. Might be best to call Harper and explain the situation. After they were through here, it'd be too late to stop by her house. There was no reason to return, anyway, except to leave her flashlight on the porch and retrieve his car from the driveway. He'd checked her home and found no cause for alarm.

He ran a hand through his hair. Damn if the night didn't feel a little colder and lonelier. He called Harper's number but got no answer. Maybe she was getting ready for bed. Liam left a voice message that he'd found a body and would be tied up the rest of the evening.

Blue lights strobed on King Street at the same moment his phone rang. Liam held the flashlight straight up in the air as a beacon and verbally guided the officers to his precise location.

"What's happening? What did you find?"

He whirled around at the familiar voice. "Thought you'd gone back to the house."

"Fat chance," Harper said, looking around the scene.

He knew the exact moment she spotted the body. She inhaled sharply. "Is he…is he—"

"Dead," he confirmed. "We have the situation covered." He briefly pressed her small, trembling hand. "Go on back," he urged.

The police car bumped along the field and parked close by. A detective and the forensics examiner exited the vehicle and immediately set to work taking pictures and putting the body in a bag while Liam filled them in on what he knew. A siren sounded in the distance, and another cop car pulled up by the small crowd. Liam frowned when he recognized the driver.

Bryce Fairfax strode over, hands on hips as he surveyed the scene. His eyes widened at the sight of Harper. "What are you doing out here?"

"We saw a light in the marsh, and Liam… Officer Andrews…wanted to check it out."

Bryce shot him a stern look. "Civilians don't need to be at a crime scene—unless they've witnessed a crime, of course."

Liam clamped his jaw tight to prevent an angry defense. His boss never failed to find something to criticize in his work. It had been like that almost since he'd transferred to the Baysville PD five months ago.

"It's not his fault," Harper said quickly. "He told me not to come out here, but I did anyway."

"So I see."

Bryce shot him another look that promised he'd speak with him later about this matter. What a jerk.

"I'll go on home," Harper said, giving Liam an apologetic smile before handing him her flashlight. "I won't need this now."

"I'll have you escorted," Chief Fairfax said, motioning to one of the responding officers.

For the next hour, they took statements and searched for forensic evidence. Bryce questioned the homeless men. His condescension was evident in his smirk and sharp, pointed questions. Bryce released them with a warning not to leave town. Liam predicted they'd be hopping the next train that passed through. Bryce had to realize that as well, which meant another unsolved vagrant murder.

"That should wrap it up for tonight, men," Bryce said, hitching up his belt and puffing out his chest. "Appears this is nothing more than another case of vagrants killing one of their own. Probably arguing over alcohol or drugs, I bet."

"You're forgetting the car," Liam pointed out. "There was someone roaming the field, and then we heard a vehicle driving off."

Bryce chuckled. "Probably just some teenagers making out. You know how kids are." He nodded at the other two men. "Sam, stay here and keep the crime scene secure until another officer arrives from the midnight shift. George, go on home now. I need to speak to Andrews."

George left with a wave, Sam resumed searching the ground and Liam was alone with his boss.

"What were you doing over at Harper Catlett's place?"

"I offered to search her house. She seemed upset this morning about the noises and that email. And someone tried to run her down with a truck. I'll be writing up a report."

Bryce popped a stick of clove chewing gum in his mouth. "Let me fill you in on Harper. Her sister, Presley, died in that house seventeen years ago. Harper was only nine at the time. She was the first one on the scene. Claimed she saw a sickly looking man—or creature—hovering over her sister and that he just disappeared into thin air. The police thoroughly searched the place. Nobody had been in that house. Nobody, you understand?"

"So she told me. What are you saying? That she lied?"

"*Lie* is a strong word. Maybe a better word is *imaginative*. After all, she was a kid. Probably woke up from a nightmare and then suffered a trauma when she saw Presley dead. Or it could have been she was thinking of the Shadow Dweller."

"The Shadow Dweller? What are you talking about?"

"A local legend. Some people—mostly kids—claim to see a filthy, emaciated creature that vanishes the instant he's spotted. They say he peeks out of house windows or deserted buildings, especially whenever the mailman passes by." Bryce chuckled. "When items go missing—a jacket, a pecan pie, a blanket—folks blame it on the Shadow Dweller."

Liam mulled over the new information. "And you think Harper's mind leaped to the legend when she found her sister?"

"Could be. Took a long time before kids stopped giving her grief about what she claimed to have seen."

"Kids can be cruel. What did her parents say about it?"

"Her dad had died a year earlier. Ruth, her mom, made Harper go to grief counseling."

A stab of sympathy shot through him. Must have

been pretty tough for Harper. "And you bring all this up because...?"

"Isn't it obvious? Again, she's claiming to hear noises in the house and that she received a threatening email. Weird how the proof happened to disappear."

Anger thrummed along his temples at the insinuation. "Harper's not crazy." He'd seen her abrasions from the near run-in with the truck. Those were real, and there had been a witness to the incident.

"Now, now. I didn't say that."

"You implied it."

"I'm merely laying out the facts for you. Might want to take what she says with a grain of salt. You found nothing in her house, correct?"

"Correct," he reluctantly admitted. "But someone did try to run her over—"

"Just watch your step, that's all I'm saying. You entered her house, still in uniform, and spent time alone with her. Use caution. Who knows what goes on in that head of hers? I don't want my department getting a harebrained sexual harassment complaint because Harper's made up some fantasy in her head about *you.*"

"Your fears are unwarranted," he said stiffly. "Doubt I'll even see her again before she leaves."

"Might be for the best."

Although it was offered as a suggestion, Liam understood his boss meant it as an order. Bryce hitched up his pants again and strolled to his car.

Alone in the marsh, Liam ran a hand through his

hair and sighed. Porch lights shone from Harper's house, and he could make out her silhouette where she stood, waiting. He'd return her flashlight and then be on his solitary way. Although he disagreed with his boss as to Harper's state of mind.

Reluctantly, he returned. Harper opened the screen door and beckoned him inside, but Liam only climbed the porch steps and held out the flashlight. "Thanks for the loan. It came in handy."

"No problem." She met him halfway on the steps and took the flashlight. "Can I offer you coffee?"

"Sorry. I need to go back to the station and write up a report. I'll be on my way."

She reached out to him, and the heat of her hand bled through his uniform sleeve. "I appreciate you coming over." An uncertain smile lit her pale face. "Thanks for taking this matter seriously. Not everyone does that for me. But you did."

"So I heard."

Harper winced. "Bryce must have filled you in on my past. That didn't take long."

"It doesn't matter what other people think."

"Easy for you to say." Harper shrugged. "It took a long time for all that stuff to blow over. Should have realized no one's forgotten it, though. Hell, I'm not sure I even believe what I saw anymore."

"I see why you want to sell this place and get back to Atlanta. Lots of bad memories here."

"And good ones from when all four of us were alive. It wasn't all bad. Guess all families are complicated that way."

"Right." He dug his car keys out of his pocket.

"Maybe I'll see you around?" she asked.

The wistful note in her voice tugged at him. "Maybe."

He turned away and started down the steps, conscious of her watching. His legs felt as though they weighed a ton. He didn't want to leave Harper. That murder had been way too close to her house, right after someone had nearly run her over, and the night grew darker by the minute. What if the murderer had seen them leave her home and head into the marsh where he'd just killed? Unlike Bryce, he didn't believe it was an instance of the homeless killing one of their own. His boss was lazy, too quick to dismiss the murders as unimportant casualties of the transients turning on one another.

Liam would never forgive himself if he left Harper alone and something happened to her. He had to do more to keep her safe.

Liam turned back to Harper. "Want to go to the store with me? I need to pick up a few things before it closes at nine."

Her face lit up. "Actually, I'm wound up too tight to relax, and I could use a few things. I'll grab my purse and meet you out front."

What Bryce didn't know wouldn't hurt him. He liked Harper, and he'd been in law enforcement for years. Not as though he were a rookie about to be taken in by a deranged woman. No, he was capable of making his own decisions about a person's character. Bryce might have distant knowledge of Harper through her sister and mutual acquaintances, but that didn't mean he knew the woman she'd become.

Soon, she stood by the vehicle, waiting with purse in hand.

"That was quick." He opened the door for her, and she slid in.

"No time to waste if we want to make it by closing."

Liam entered the driver's side and started the engine.

"Is your fridge totally empty?" Harper asked. "That happens to me all the time in Atlanta. I'll work long hours and forget to shop. I end up eating way too much fast food."

"The groceries aren't for me."

She shot him a questioning glance as he backed out of the driveway.

"It's for the men we met tonight," he admitted reluctantly. "Gunner, I guess you could call him their leader, mentioned they'd been searching for the victim. They'd scraped together money for him to buy provisions for a stew tonight."

"You're buying the food for them? You're a kind man."

Liam shifted uncomfortably in his seat at her look of admiration. He shrugged. "It's no big deal. I have a soft spot for the homeless. My uncle used to be one. For all I know, maybe he still is. We haven't heard from him in years."

"That's terrible. Were you close?"

"Not me, but my mother was close to Uncle Teddy.

She still harbors an irrational hope of reuniting with him one day." Liam crossed an intersection, bemused at his admission. He didn't normally open up to people so quickly.

"Anything's possible. He might turn up one day out of the blue."

"I've asked around about him, of course. Over a decade ago, he was arrested several times in Baysville for public vagrancy and for living in abandoned buildings. After the last arrest, he spent a few nights in the county jail. Probably a welcome change from cold and hunger. Never was seen or heard from again. I've showed old photos of my uncle to Gunner and some of the older guys, but they didn't recognize him."

"At least you tried. I'm sure your mom appreciates that."

They fell into a comfortable silence as he drove through town. A few couples strolled the river walk, and others exited from the main street restaurants that were closing. The scent of crab cakes and lobster was strong enough to detect even in the car. One of the many advantages of living in a tourist town were the great restaurants and bars.

He'd be sad to leave when the time came. His stint in Baysville was temporary, although his boss and coworkers didn't know that. Only one person knew his real reason for coming, and Liam trusted him to keep that knowledge secret.

"This seems like a great place to grow up," he noted.

"Mostly. If only…well, if only Presley hadn't had

that accident and I hadn't seen what I did." She hesitated. "Or what I thought I saw."

"Can you describe it again? In more detail?"

"A man hovered over Presley. Extremely pale. When he looked up at me, I couldn't really read his expression. His eyes were large and full of contradiction—anger, surprise, but mostly fear. Although he couldn't have been more afraid of me than I was of him."

"How tall was he?"

"Hard to say since he was bent over, but I don't think he was a tall man. He wore dirty clothes that were ragged, and his face and arms looked as though they were crusted in dirt. If not for that, he might have been glow-in-the-dark pale. Very sickly looking."

"The legendary Shadow Dweller, perhaps?"

The corners of her mouth turned down. "Bryce was awfully chatty tonight, wasn't he? And here I thought he was my friend—that we shared a connection through Presley's memory."

A false belief like that could be dangerous. He shouldn't say anything, and yet... "A word of warning," he said reluctantly. "Don't trust Bryce Fairfax one hundred percent. He might not be all that he appears to be on the surface."

Chapter Four

She should be tired. Bone weary after the night's events. Instead, Harper tossed underneath the covers. Even when she wasn't consciously listening for an out-of-place sound, her brain remained on high alert. So far, coming home hadn't eradicated her fear of old ghosts and things that went bump in the night. Yet, she owed it to herself to stay and confront the memories head-on. With each bit of clothing donated or trash discarded, with the stripping away of each material possession tied to the house, Harper hoped to sweep away the remaining cobwebs of mystery and sadness.

Sighing, she admitted defeat. No matter how much she needed eight hours of shut-eye, sleep eluded her. Experience taught her that when all else failed—a hot bath, yoga, warm milk and a misting diffuser of lavender essential oil—the best remedy was to read the most boring material available. Harper climbed out of bed, strolled to her mom's bedroom and emptied out a drawerful of old papers from her desk. Might as well kill two birds with one stone, get rid of

outdated paperwork and read until her eyes became
so blurry she'd be forced to close them and drift off
to never-never land.

She carried a stack of papers to the bed, fluffed a
pillow behind her back and dug in. Outdated checks,
old warranties and instruction manuals—Mom was
clearly old-school and didn't trust keeping records
on a computer. But two-thirds of the way through
the stack, an official government record caught her
attention.

Her breath caught at the heading: Autopsy Report
of Presley Lee Catlett. The yellowed sheet of paper
shook beneath her trembling fingers as she read on.
"Cause of death: Asphyxiation from severe spinal
cord injury at the fourth cervical vertebra." Para-
graphs of further medical description continued, de-
scribing the damaged tissue on the base of Presley's
skull and trauma to internal organs, all consistent
with smoke asphyxiation. "Other findings: Deceased
was nine weeks pregnant. Signed, Dr. Thomas J.
Lumpkin, Pathologist."

Pregnant? In stunned disbelief, Harper slapped
the report against her thighs. "Presley was pregnant?" she squeaked in the silent room, as if someone was nearby and could respond. Why hadn't her
mother ever mentioned it? Harper stood and paced,
running a hand through her tousled hair. She'd imagined herself all cried out years ago, but a fresh well
of grief burst inside. Nine weeks, so her sister had
to have known about her condition before her unexpected death.

And so had Mom. Yet she'd never mentioned a word of it to Harper. Why not? Did she imagine shielding her from the news would make her sister's death any less painful?

Who else knew about this? Did the biological father know? Harper abruptly stopped pacing, recalling Presley's old boyfriend, Allen Spencer. They'd broken up days before Presley's accident. She hadn't thought much of it at the time, but now she couldn't help wondering. Did Allen break up with Presley when, or if, she told him about the pregnancy?

A sliver of muted light shone through the lace curtain. Another day dawning. And yes, learning about the pregnancy made Presley's early death even more tragic.

Would Presley have kept the baby? Harper rather thought her sister was the kind of girl who would do just that. And maybe, just maybe, that had enraged her ex-boyfriend. Maybe even enough to kill her.

Harper crawled back in bed and rubbed her temples. Allen was no killer. The man was a well-respected preacher now, had been for many years. Last she'd heard, he was married with three kids. Besides, whatever she'd seen or not seen that night, it certainly wasn't Allen.

She had to get out of the suddenly stifling house. The only place open this early in the morning would be the Dixie Diner, Mom's old place of employment. A chocolate crème–filled doughnut and a vanilla latte would provide a welcome sugary distraction. On a whim, Harper whipped out her cell phone and texted Kimber to see if her old friend had time to join her calorie fest.

She was in luck. Kimber agreed to meet her there in thirty minutes.

"I CAN'T BELIEVE that murder last night was so close to you," Kimber said with a shudder. "Practically in your own backyard."

Rhoda, a waitress, hovered nearby, smoothing her hands over her apron. "Heard about it on the radio this morning. Not what you needed after all you've been through." She patted Harper's shoulder in sympathy before returning to wait tables.

"Did you see or hear anything?" Kimber asked.

"I'd rather not talk about it."

Kimber nodded. "Okay. I get it. If you change your mind later, give me a buzz."

Harper soaked in the sweet, heady scent of chocolate, coffee and fresh-baked doughnuts that permeated every square inch of the rustic diner, which sported turquoise Formica tabletops, waitresses in white aprons and local folks sipping white mugs of steaming coffee. It was like stepping into a 1950s soda shop. Even the windows were clouded with condensation, and Harper imagined herself embraced in a cozy cocoon of warm deliciousness. Just what she needed after last night.

"Here ya go, honey," Rhoda said, returning with Harper's food and drink. She patted Harper's shoulder. "I think of your mom every day." The two had worked the morning shift together for nearly three decades. She shook her head, her gray curls straining against a black hairnet. "Keep expecting her to breeze through the door any minute and put on her apron." Rhoda turned to Kimber. "What'll it be this morning, sweetheart?"

"Toast and black coffee." Kimber smiled at Harper's wince as Rhoda sauntered to the kitchen. "What can I say? I've been on a perpetual diet since having kids."

"You look great," Harper assured her. And she did. Kimber was a tall, cool blonde with terrific bone structure and a homecoming queen aura, even if she'd finished high school eons ago. Smart, too. Owned a successful real estate company and ruled her roost of husband and three kids with an easy aplomb that Harper couldn't help but admire.

"How's the house prep coming along?" Kimber asked. "Don't forget, I have a cleaning crew that can make short work of it for you. Reasonable rates."

Harper waved a dismissive hand. "I remember. I need to go through a lot myself, but after that, I'll give them a call. Text me their info."

Kimber nodded. "I understand. Lots of old memories tied up in the place. How much longer you reckon it'll take? Aren't you worried about your business in Atlanta?"

"I'm going to call my assistant today and have her take over a couple of outstanding jobs. She can contact future customers and explain there'll be a short delay due to a family emergency."

"I'm sure they'll understand. Just give me the

word when you're ready to place your house on the market. It might be difficult—it's an older home—but I'm the best."

"Even after what happened to Presley in the house?" she asked doubtfully.

"It won't be the first home I've sold where tragic accidents have occurred, so even though it's an obstacle, I know how to overcome it. Not all agents do." Kimber laughed. "Not that I'm trying to rush you for a commission. Hell, I wish you'd move back to Baysville." Her classically sculpted face grew pensive. "I could use a friend."

"You?" She scoffed, surprised at Kimber's words. "You've got plenty of friends. You've lived here all your life."

"Mmm-hmm," she murmured, not revealing anything. "But small towns can be lonely places."

Harper frowned at Kimber's uncharacteristic vulnerability. "Is something wrong?"

Kimber folded her hands on the table and gave a tight smile. "Not at all. Just an off kind of morning."

She studied her friend's blue eyes—the exact shade of Pagan River's navy hue. Harper had always viewed it as a sign that Kimber perfectly fit in with Baysville. But what did one ever really know of another person's secret trials? Presley had carried a huge secret on her teenage shoulders, without a word to anyone, as far as Harper could tell. Weren't small towns supposed to be an open book where everybody knew everybody's history and where gossip ran rampant?

But not a word of Presley's pregnancy had been whispered about in the grapevine. Not that had gotten back to her, at any rate. Harper leaned forward, keeping her voice low. "Have you ever heard any rumors about Presley?"

Kimber blinked. "What kind of rumors? I mean, she's been dead for years."

"Before she died, did you ever hear talk of anything about her, um, sex life?"

"She dated Allen Spencer. Whether they slept together, I haven't a clue. Why do you ask?"

Harper silently debated. What did it really matter after all these years? But Presley had kept her secret, and it didn't seem right to spill the beans now. "Never mind. It's not important. I've been going through old family stuff and it's made me maudlin, I suppose."

"Understandable. Your sister always kind of kept to herself. But I remember Presley as smart and very likable. Just don't put her on a pedestal, though… after all, she was very young. Whatever it is you've found, if Presley was less than perfect, so what?" Kimber lightened the mood with a wink. "The two of us did plenty of questionable things as teenagers."

"True enough. Guess I'm in an off mood as well. My house is still…unsettling."

"The memories?" she asked sympathetically.

"Yeah. And other things… Sounds, senses… something. I know there has to be a logical explanation, but it gets to me." Kimber was the only one she could talk to about it. Everyone else either shut her out or stared at her with eyes full of pity. She hated that look.

"Here y'all go." Rhoda set down their food and drink. "Enjoy."

"Breakfast of champions," Harper grinned, biting into the doughnut.

Kimber stoically bit into her dry toast and downed it with a sip of black coffee. "I'm glad you texted about meeting this morning. There's something I've been meaning to ask you."

Harper raised her brows and kept eating.

"I have a proposition for you." Kimber straightened, assuming her professional Realtor mantle. "As I said, your house presents certain challenges to a sale. Even though I know I could meet them, there's a simpler solution to its marketability issues—I'd like to buy it."

"Why?" She was taken aback at the offer. Kimber and Joe lived in a rambling old farmhouse outside town that they'd renovated into a showcase. It was her pride and joy. "Thought you loved your farmhouse."

"Oh, we do. We have no plans to move. Your house would be an investment. I've studied the market carefully, and I believe I could turn it into a profitable bed-and-breakfast."

An unexpected twinge of sadness swept through her. "You know, that's what Dad always wanted to do with the place. Mom had started to warm to the idea before Presley died. She gave up on dreams after that."

"I remember. That's what gave me the idea. Besides making a nice profit, I figured it would be a blessing for you as well. A win-win. I'd buy it immediately, and you could return to Atlanta without worrying about selling it." Kimber's face brightened with enthusiasm. "Not only would the house be in good hands, but also it'd bring your dad's dream to light."

All true, so why didn't the arrangement make her happy?

Kimber's smile dimmed. "What's wrong? You don't like the idea?"

"It's just unexpected."

Kimber patted her hand. "If you don't want to, no hard feelings. But think about it, okay? And, of course, I'd hire you to do all the decorating. That way, you'll always have a presence there. Might even entice you to visit Baysville more often if you could spend the night in your old home."

"You're the best, Kimber. Let me consider it for a few days, and I'll let you know."

"Of course."

She still wasn't sold, which made no sense. Her friend's offer would hasten cutting all ties to her hometown. Wasn't that what she wanted? More people bustled in the diner, grabbing breakfast or coffee before heading to work. Several uniformed officers entered, and she recognized Liam and Bryce heading to the counter. At the sight of Liam's tall figure, her heart kicked up its heels.

Kimber's cell phone buzzed, and she picked it up, a slight frown tugging her face. "Business calls," she said crisply. "I've got an unexpected client meeting. Sorry, I've got to run."

"No problem. Quick question, though. This cleaning crew of yours, can they handle large jobs?"

"They've done everything from hauling off old furniture in vacated houses to fire damage renovation. Nothing's too big or too small."

Harper dug the spare house key out of her purse and slid it across the table to Kimber. "Consider them hired. I need a good set of muscles to haul off all of Dad's old tools and benches in the basement. They can donate anything in good condition to charity and dump the rest. Stop by anytime and go down there to assess the fee. I don't need to be home."

"I'll do it today," Kimber promised. After they made a dinner date for later in the week, she bustled off. Harper watched through the window as she quickly walked to her car and climbed inside. Sell the house to Kimber? She tried to convince herself to accept the offer. It was the rational move to make, and yet...

"Harper?" Liam approached her booth. "May I join you?"

"Please do." He slid in opposite her, and his gray eyes bored into hers, as if he could read all her secrets.

Bryce stopped by the booth. "Morning, Harper. Any more threatening emails or unexplained noises?"

Several customers shifted their gazes to them, and her face warmed. Did he have to boom out the question within earshot of so many people? "Not in the past twenty-four hours."

"Good, good. We're always here if you need us. You coming, Andrews?"

"In a few minutes."

A look passed between them, a tiny beat of tension. "Don't stay too long—we've got a full load today." Bryce turned from Liam to her and rapped his hand on the table. "See you around, then. Hopefully not in my official capacity."

She sipped her drink, relieved to find the other patrons resuming their own conversations. Liam leaned in, keeping his voice low. "You sure you're going to be okay? You look…weary."

"I didn't get much sleep last night," she admitted. "I kept thinking about that poor guy killed nearby. I tried to tackle a project, to get my mind off the murder, but I read something in Mom's old papers that disturbed me."

"Want to talk about it?"

The loud rev of an engine distracted her. Outside, Bryce backed a police cruiser out of his parking place. "Don't you need to get to the station? What with the full load Bryce mentioned."

"No hurry." Liam kept his eyes pinned on her.

Somehow, she found herself telling him about the autopsy report. Strange how she felt so free to confide in him instead of her longtime best friend. Maybe because he never knew her sister, it felt like less of a betrayal to confide about the pregnancy.

"Damn, what a horrible way to find out."

"I can't believe Mom never told me."

"She might have been trying to protect you from more pain."

"Probably. But I wish she had talked to me. Mom shut down after Presley's death. Her life became a matter of merely going through the motions of living."

"Do you think this report has any bearing on your sister's death—on what you saw that night?"

"No. Her boyfriend, Allen Spencer, looks nothing like whatever I saw on the staircase. Although—I do wonder if Allen knew." She set down her drink. The sugary sweetness that had tasted so good going down now roiled in her belly.

"I can ask him for you."

"Seriously? You don't think that would be presumptuous? I barely know the guy, and you don't know him at all. Won't you get into trouble for asking about his teenage behavior—wouldn't he think you were harassing him?"

"It's all in the approach. I'll tell him I'm searching for answers about what happened to Presley since some new information has come up. It's the truth."

"He's a minister now. He's sure to be taken aback by you questioning him and his reputation. Let me do it. At least I won't be a stranger."

"I don't know…"

"He's a minister. He knew my sister. Knew of her tragic death. Surely he'll respond with compassion."

"All right. But I'll go with you. Not in an official

capacity. I'll change into my civilian clothes but let you do all the talking."

His kindness tugged at her heart, yet an ugly suspicion arose inside. Why was he being so helpful? He barely knew her. "Why?" she asked abruptly.

"Why what?"

"Why are you being so nice?"

"Maybe I'm just a decent guy."

Of course, that was one explanation. Why must she always be so suspicious of people's motives? If alive, Mom would advise her not to look a gift horse in the mouth. "Okay, let's do this. When's a good time for you?"

"When I get off work this evening. Find out the minister's schedule, and we'll work something out." Liam finished the last of his coffee and set it down. "One last word of advice—don't warn him we're coming."

She hadn't expected that. "Why not?"

"He might not have been the man you saw that night, but say he and your sister argued about the pregnancy. Maybe she wanted to keep the baby, and that infuriated him. Enough so that he hired someone to hurt her."

"A teenager hiring a hit man? Bit of a stretch, I think."

"I've seen it all in my line of work. Never underestimate what people will do when they're in a rage or feel cornered. By the way, I filed the report on that truck that came at you. Nothing's come up yet, but I'll let you know if something does." Liam slid out of the booth. "I'll buzz you later."

She continued to sit for a few more minutes, pondering Liam's parting salvo. The Allen she remembered had been a quiet, slightly nerdy kind of guy. But what was that old line about how you always have to watch the quiet ones?

"You doing okay, sweetie? More coffee?" Rhoda appeared at her side, a fresh pot in her hands.

"No, thanks. I'd better get going." Harper slapped a generous tip on the table and eased out of the booth, only now noticing several people standing at the entrance, waiting on a clean table. No wonder Mom used to come home with aching feet and a sore back from serving a steady stream of customers.

She waved goodbye to the staff and headed outside, gazing forlornly at her car. Everyone else seemed so busy and content, full of things to do and people to meet. The way she had been not so long ago. And now? Nothing waiting on her but a creepy house that still needed more cleaning and decluttering. She didn't even want to return to her childhood home—how sad was that? If she had any sense, she'd call Kimber immediately and accept her offer to buy it. In two days, she could be back at her old job in Atlanta, slipping into a comfortable routine.

Funny how that hardly appealed to her, either.

Harper pushed her shoulders back and strode forward. The thing was to keep busy. She'd sleep on Kimber's offer tonight and call her in the morning with a decision.

"Harper? Harper Catlett?"

The deep, booming voice sounded familiar. She swung around, spotting Captain Carlton Fairfax bearing down on her. Make that ex-captain. Bryce's father was a negative image of his son. Where Bryce was muscular, Carlton was stocky. Bryce's dark good looks and affable smile managed to look downright smarmy on his dad, although the family resemblance was there in the strong jaw and in the confident aura both exuded.

He held out a beefy hand, and she shook it, almost wincing at his tight squeeze. Was that a male dominance tactic—show her who was stronger? There she went with the suspicions again.

"Knew it had to be you with the wild red hair." He grinned.

She forced a smile, reminding herself that he had been kind to her and Mom after the accident. Not to mention he'd been the first responder at the scene that night and had whisked them away to safety.

"Sorry about your mother. She was a good woman, that Ruth. A hard worker."

"Yes, sir."

"Reckon you'll be heading out of Baysville in the next few days?"

She felt a perverse desire to contradict his assumption. "I might just stay." The admission surprised even her.

His smile slipped a notch. "I'd have thought Baysville wouldn't hold much attraction to a young lady with a fancy decorating career in Atlanta."

It almost sounded as though he wanted her to leave. "Isn't the mayor your buddy? Don't imagine he'd find your portrayal of Baysville very flattering."

He barked out a laugh but hardly appeared amused. Harper opened her car door. "Good to see you again." She shut herself inside, ending the conversation. From the rearview mirror, she saw him watch her as she backed out of the parking space and then onto Main Street. His stare was oddly unsettling. Probably a guilt by association thing. Since Liam had warned her that Bryce might not be a particularly reliable person, she assumed his dad was cut from the same cloth. It felt odd to be wary of them when she'd looked up to Bryce as a girl. But she was starting to view him in a different light now, especially since he'd refused to take her fears seriously.

She turned on the radio, determined to shake off her uneasy mood. Obviously, last night's discovery still played on her emotions, too, making her mistrustful of everyone and their motives. For now, she'd concentrate on her upcoming interview with the preacher.

Chapter Five

The nearly deserted church had an eerie vibe. On either side of the main sanctuary, the rippled surface of stained-glass windows sparkled like deep-hued jewels in the waning sunlight. A weighty silence blanketed the room, as though thousands of prayers were compressed between the walls.

From a distance came the sound of a girl's high-pitched voice—out of place and jarring. Liam couldn't make out the words, but he guessed from her tone that she was agitated.

"The youth group always met in the basement on Thursday nights," Harper said in a near whisper. "If memory serves, it should begin in about fifteen minutes. When I called earlier, the church secretary told me that Allen personally conducts their meetings and would be available."

"Hmm...so he knows we're coming?"

"If the secretary told him. I know you didn't want to alert him to our visit, but she asked if I wanted to see him."

"No problem. The basement it is, then." Liam

nodded, amused that he'd also lowered his voice, as though conversing in a normal tone would violate the reverent atmosphere. "I meant to ask, did Allen conduct the funeral service for your mother?"

"No, we went to a different church across town."

They stepped from the sanctuary into a dimly lit hallway lined with rows of closed doors with placards designating various Bible study groups. A sliver of light shone from the last door on the right, casting a patchwork of shadows on the linoleum floor.

"Allen? Where are you?"

That same querulous voice he'd heard in the sanctuary drew closer, emerging from the staircase to his left. A young girl rounded the second level of the stairs, blinking at them in surprise. Skinny and with a short pixie cut feathering her face, her eyes looked impossibly large.

"We're looking for him, too." Harper veered from his side and walked toward the stairs. "Are you part of the youth group?"

"Yes, ma'am. Sort of."

A muffled rustling sounded from down the hallway, much more interesting than this conversation with the girl. Liam quietly padded toward the occupied room, tuning in to whispering voices and the unmistakable metallic clicking of a zipper. He reckoned he'd either found the missing preacher or two brazen teenagers who'd arrived early for the youth meeting and decided to engage in a little fun first.

The doorknob turned, and a fortysomething man appeared, running a hand through his short hair, his reading glasses slightly askew on his delicate features. He pasted on a nervous smile. "Did I hear someone calling for me?"

"Allen Spencer?" Liam asked.

Allen quickly shut the door behind him and walked away as if in a hurry to get somewhere. "Yes? Do I know you?"

"Where ya been?" The teenager pushed in front of Liam to confront Allen, eyes narrowed.

Now wasn't this all very interesting. The man was hiding a secret. If he had a consensual thing going on with an adult employee, Liam couldn't pursue that in any official way. But the inappropriate flash of suspicion and jealousy in the teenager's eyes gave him pause. Did Allen flirt with these young girls and lead them on? Perhaps something even worse was happening here.

"Patience, Kristen." Allen frowned a warning at the girl before catching sight of Harper. He squinted and tentatively offered his hand, ignoring Liam. "Aren't you—"

"Harper Catlett. Presley's sister."

They shook hands. "Yes, yes. There's a resemblance. I heard about your mother. So sorry. What brings you here tonight?"

Liam's suspicion increased as the preacher drew them toward his office—and away from the closed door of the Adult Disciples room. Harper glanced at him with raised brows, a silent acknowledgment that she was also aware of the man's odd behavior. Allen flipped on the lights and bade them enter, motioning them to sit on the couch across from his desk. "Come in, come in. I only have a few minutes, though, before the youth group starts. Kristen, will you please go downstairs and set up the chairs for me?"

Kristen pouted, and Liam thought she was about to refuse, but the girl huffed out of the room, producing a surprising amount of noise as she stomped down the stairs. Liam remained standing at the door while Harper seated herself.

Allen perched behind the desk, folding his slender fingers together atop its mahogany surface. "This must be a difficult time for you after losing your mother," he began in what sounded to Liam like practiced, professional rote. "But death is not really the end, it's—"

"Thank you, but that's not why I'm here," Harper interrupted.

"Oh?" Surprise lit behind the thick lens of his glasses.

The landline phone on his desk rang, and he winced. "Excuse me a moment. I never know when it might be someone in the congregation who needs my assistance."

Perfect timing. Liam raised a finger toward Harper. "Be right back," he murmured.

She nodded in understanding. Allen appeared wrapped up in his phone call. Liam closed the door behind him and made his way back down the hall. If he found a grown woman trying to discreetly slip away, then there wasn't much he could do if she was part of a consensual affair. It would make Allen a hypocrite and adulterer, but not necessarily a law-breaker. If, however, the man was fooling around with underage girls, that was a different story entirely. Allen was in serious trouble in that case. At the last room on the right, from which Allen had originally emerged, he quickly opened the door and stepped inside.

All was quiet. A corner lamp softly lit the unoccupied room where a circle of metal folding chairs was arranged. On the walls were shelves of books and angel statues. Had he missed whoever had been there a minute earlier? "It's okay, you can come out now."

From the corner of his eye, he caught a slight movement to his far left. There. A young girl's head peeked out from behind the back of a large, wing-backed chair positioned near the back window. They silently, warily eyed one another.

"Who are you?" she whispered.

Automatically, his right hand reached for the back pocket that held his wallet and police identification. He thought better of it. The girl was nervous enough without throwing that bit of information into the mix right off the bat.

"Liam Andrews," he answered simply. "Come on out."

She emerged from behind the chair, nervously running her hands through her shoulder-length tangle of curls. "I, um, I'd lost an earring and was looking for it."

"In that case, it might have been helpful to turn on the overhead light."

"Yeah." She gave a self-deprecating giggle and stuffed her hands in the front pockets of her jeans. "You're right. My bad."

He commanded her gaze. "How'd you lose the earring?"

She lifted her shoulders and raised her palms in a whatcha-gonna-do gesture. "Oh, you know..." The girl shuffled past him, her head bent low.

"Hold on there," he said.

She spun around. "Yes, sir?"

"How old are you?"

"Fifteen. Why?"

A minor then. This was bad. "What was going on in here?"

"Wh-what do you mean?" A blush scoured her cheeks even as guilt flashed in her wide green eyes. Her hands left her pockets, and she again played with the loose curls framing her girlish face.

"You can tell me. I'm a cop. I'll help you."

Her eyes darted to the door.

"Would you rather discuss this with a female officer?" he asked gently. "I can call someone in."

White teeth scraped at her bottom lip. Slowly, she started walking backward toward the exit door. "I'm, um, late. I gotta go."

"What's your name?"

"Mary Smith."

If he wasn't so concerned for her, he'd have been angry at the blatant lie. "What's going on here is wrong," he said gently. "Like I said, I can help you. But I need your real name. And your parents' phone number."

Mary—or whatever her name was—visibly paled, and her mouth dropped open in fear. She bolted.

Liam rushed into the hallway after her as she streaked through the sanctuary, swift as a scared bunny.

Allen's study door opened, and he poked his head out, furtively scanning the hallway. "Everything okay out here? Emily, what's going on?" he called after the girl.

Harper pushed past Allen and joined him in the pursuit.

"Emily, wait!" she pleaded. She looked back at Liam, and said softly, "She might talk to a woman."

The girl halted and peered over her shoulder.

"Can we talk a minute?" Harper asked, approaching her slowly, holding out a hand. "Just you and me."

Allen caught up to them, huffing from the short run. "Why are you running, Emily? What's going on?"

Liam's jaw clenched at the man's faked air of innocence and the deliberate, warning frown he gave the young girl. He stepped in front of Allen, blocking his view of Emily. "Harper, do you mind taking Emily inside while I deal with Mr. Spencer?"

"What do you say, Emily?" Harper smiled softly, draped an arm over the girl's shoulder and guided her to the sanctuary. "Everything's going to be fine, honey. You'll see."

Thank heavens for Harper's assistance. The arrest would be so much easier without the victim witnessing it and possibly trying to protect her abuser, denying that anything wrong had occurred.

"Get in my car," he ordered Spencer. "I'm taking you into the station for questioning."

"Questioning? Wh-what are you talking about?"

"I'm a cop. It's my job to investigate this." Liam took a grim satisfaction at Allen's widened eyes and the sudden slump of his shoulders. He stepped forward, his face within inches of Allen's—close enough to smell his sweat, even through the mentholated scent of the man's aftershave.

"But I haven't done anything wrong," he protested, clear blue eyes awash with barely contained panic. "You can't make me go."

"Get in the car."

Allen's shoulders slumped as he complied with the order. Liam caught up to Harper and pulled her aside from Emily. "Just wait with Emily in an empty room and don't discuss anything with her about what just happened. I'm calling in an officer who specializes in this kind of possible crime, and she'll talk to Emily about the matter."

Harper nodded. "I understand. Don't worry."

Liam called in to the station and arranged for an officer to come over and speak with Emily at once. He returned to his car and confronted Allen. "Here's what's going to happen," he said shortly. "An expert officer in the field is going to interview Emily. Whatever was going on in there, it's all going to come out.

I suggest you tell the truth. Now. It might go easier on you that way."

"I was counseling that girl. How dare you! What will my parishioners think? You'll ruin my reputation."

Liam continued. "Didn't you hear me? Admit to everything now."

Allen shook his head, as though dazed. "This can't be happening. Please. I was counseling Emily. Nothing inappropriate happened."

"Really? And that's why you were in a dimly lit room with her behind closed doors?"

"I can assure you that—"

"We practically caught you in the act."

"You have no proof," he insisted. Allen's skin looked ashen, and he licked his thin lips. "Okay, I'll admit that my behavior has been somewhat inappropriate, but I've never crossed a certain line—"

Disgust filled Liam. "She's a minor. You admit to having physical contact with her of a sexual nature?"

"Yeah, but like I said, we never actually—"

"You're under arrest," Liam interrupted. "I'm taking you to the station."

Allen started to tremble. "My reputation will be in ruins. I'll lose my job."

"Should have thought about that before you crossed the line with a minor. Now stay in here a minute until I return."

Liam made his way into the church and followed the sound of low murmurs coming from Allen's office. Harper and Emily glanced up at him as he entered. Emily's face was tearstained, and her hands shook as she swiped a tissue at her eyes. Harper stood, patting the girl's shoulder as she exited the room and slipped beside him in the hallway.

"What's going on?" she asked. "Did you arrest Allen?"

"I did. How's Emily?"

"She's seems scared to death and called her parents, who, by the way, are on their way over."

"Good. You didn't speak to her about anything that happened?"

"I didn't."

"Excellent. I'm taking Spencer to the station. An officer should be arriving here momentarily. We'll make arrangements to get you a ride home."

"Don't worry about me." Harper crossed her arms and glanced at Emily. "What happens next? I find it hard to believe Emily is his only victim. Maybe Kristen needs to be interviewed as well."

"We'll thoroughly investigate."

"Thank heavens. That man needs to be stopped."

"I agree. Did you get to question him about your sister?"

"Yes, but I didn't learn anything. You just do what you have to do tonight, and I'll see you later."

He nodded and returned to his vehicle, his mind teeming with questions. Could there really be a connection between Presley's pregnancy and her death? He wished he could talk it over with a colleague, but that was way too risky. Word could get back to Bryce and his boss would have yet another reason to dislike him. Already, he probably skated on thin ice with tonight's arrest of a prominent citizen. Bryce would worry about how his department looked if the charges against Spencer didn't stick. The Baysville police chief was hung up on public image, his officers following a strict chain of command, and he exerted control over every facet of the department. So far, Liam hadn't been able to uncover whether this was due to the man's insecure personality or whether it was an attempt to cover up wrongdoing.

As always, the reminder of why he was really in Baysville set him on edge. Did he really want to get involved in Harper's need to poke around in her past? After all, how serious could she be about finding the truth when she was only going to be in town such a short time?

Yet every time he saw Harper, the more he liked her, the more he wanted to be close to her—and not just for official business. She was kind and intelligent and cared about people in the community. He'd just have to keep a tight rein on his emotions until the questions surrounding her sister's death and the truck that had tried to run her down were either resolved or dismissed. Spending more time with her was probably not a good idea—personally or professionally.

But he'd never been one to shy away from trouble. It was obvious Bryce had no interest in looking into Presley Catlett's death or the truck incident, and he felt like both deserved an investigation. Wherever his attraction to Harper might lead, it would have to be put on hold for now. Which might be easier said than done.

Chapter Six

Harper smiled with pleasure at the sight of Liam on her doorstep the next morning. "I was hoping you'd come by today," she said, gesturing him inside.

He held up a hand. "Sorry, I can't stay. I was in the area and just wanted to ask what, in particular, Spencer said to you about your sister when you questioned him last night."

"I didn't get much of anything out of him." She strode to the porch swing and patted the seat beside her. After a moment of hesitation, Liam sat beside her.

"I can't stop thinking about poor Emily. Hope she's the only victim."

"That would surprise me if she was. Sexual predators rarely fixate on one person."

Harper still couldn't get her head around Allen as a criminal. Maybe sexual misconduct wasn't the only violent secret in his closet. She shook her head. "At any rate, while you were out of the room, I told Allen about the autopsy report revealing Presley was pregnant. He claimed they were never intimate, even saying they had broken up a good two or three weeks before Presley died and that they'd never been serious."

"Do you believe him?" Liam asked.

"I don't know what to believe anymore. Mom always insisted on meeting Presley's dates, not that she dated that much. Matter of fact, Allen was one of only three guys I can recall Presley introducing to us."

"If you ask me, it sounds like his complete denial was too quick."

"Guess we'll never know for sure." She drummed her fingers on her lap a moment and then admitted in a rush of breath, "I've never mentioned it to anyone before, but I used to hear Presley sneaking out of the house after Mom went to bed at night."

"Think she was meeting Allen?"

"It's what I always assumed. I asked her about it, but she claimed she was just hanging out with a couple girlfriends. I never believed her story."

"How often did this happen?"

Harper cocked her head to the side, thinking. "As far as I know, only a few times. All occurring in the weeks right before her death."

"What—"

The two-way radio crackled and spit out a message.

"Duty calls," Liam said. "Let's put our heads together later and figure out our next step."

"Sure. Was that an emergency call?"

"No."

He didn't volunteer any more information, and she regarded him quizzically. She imagined having a serious relationship with a cop would be filled with moments such as this—worry every time they were called out to a scene.

"Hope everything's routine on the call."

He nodded, and she watched as he returned to his vehicle and sped off. Mrs. Henley waved her over, and Harper walked to her neighbor's house, chatting with her for over an hour before finally returning home.

That smell.

The stench wafted through the foyer—putrid and acrid, a mixture of something rotten mixed with sweat and urine. But the worst part? She'd smelled it before. That horrible night. Even over the acrid tinge of smoke, when whoever or whatever had been there brushed against her to escape into the shadows, an odor had momentarily pervaded. A very distinctive miasma of stink that triggered a gag instinct.

Harper lifted the hem of her T-shirt and covered her mouth and nose, blinking against the insistent tang. She tentatively entered the kitchen, scanning the room to determine the cause of the smell. Had something crawled in the house and died? She could think of no other explanation. The floor and counter were as she'd left them earlier—clean and wiped down. No left-out food, spilled milk or dirty dishes in the sink. The day's garbage had already been taken out. Pinching her nose, she thrust open the kitchen window. The chilly October air she could handle, not so much the smell.

Her search continued room by room. Along the way, she flung open windows and kept breathing through her mouth. And still no explanation to account for it. Upstairs, the smell dwindled to a tolerable level. In her bedroom, Harper wrapped herself in a fleece robe and opened every window before turning to the bed for the throw blanket she always kept neatly folded at the end of the mattress. Next step would be to light candles and spray every inch downstairs with air freshener. Huddling under the warm fleece blanket, she opened her night table drawer in search of a candle and matches. It was then that she noticed it—a yellowed sheet of paper scribbled with her mother's handwriting. How did it get here? Forgetting everything else, Harper sank on the bed and began reading. The letter was addressed to her mother's sister and dated three months after Presley's death.

Dear Ana,

Every day, just as I begin to believe things couldn't possibly get worse, they do. The autopsy record arrived in the mail today. It held one whopper of a surprise. Presley was pregnant. I hardly know what to think. It makes it all the more sad. Lately, it feels like I'm holding on by a thread. I'm unraveling inside. Maybe… maybe it's even affecting my mind? I'm hearing things, sis. Strange noises in the night that keep me awake. I tell myself it's because of what Harper claimed she saw that night, but I don't have the strength to figure it out.

I wish I could just pick up and move out of this place. Go somewhere like Florida where the sun always shines and the beaches glisten with white sand. My hope is that someday Harper will have a better life, far from this town with all its bittersweet memories. But I can't afford to leave. Instead, I work my butt off at the diner and dread coming home in the evenings to my mostly empty house, where the only other person there cries nearly as much as I do. I know what you'll say—to be strong for the only daughter I have left. I'm trying. I really am. But I'm a shell with nothing more to give, and I suspect Harper picks up on that.

The letter ended there. Unfinished, unsigned and undelivered. Her mom hadn't written anything Harper didn't already know, but still. Anger and hurt warred within her heart. Twin emotions both caused by the pain of realizing that her mom had no love left to give once her husband and oldest child had died. It was as though she'd grown up in a foster home with no parents to provide love or security.

She crumpled the aging paper in her fist and flung it on the floor. Anger won out over sorrow and she marched downstairs, sprayed air freshener and then gathered candles and lit them in every room.

There had to be a rational explanation. Yes, the

odor had been particularly strong the night Presley died, but every now and then the same mysterious stench of something rotten had appeared over the years, although very faint. Thank heavens the exterminators were arriving in the morning. She'd made the appointment after settling on a local business with great online reviews. Between that and getting rid of all the old possessions in the house, the problem would be removed—or at least, it wouldn't be her problem to deal with anymore. If she had any sense, she'd call Kimber right now and accept her offer.

I have nothing left to give.

Her mom's words echoed round and round in Harper's mind until a tight knot of anger balled in her gut. Presley's death had been tragic, and heartbreaking for Mom, but damn it, she was a victim in all this, too. Her childhood had sputtered to an end. If for no other reason than to satisfy her own questions, she was staying on in Baysville until she either figured out if foul play was involved in her sister's death or accepted it as truly accidental.

Decision made, Harper called her assistant in Atlanta and talked over taking an extended leave of absence. Muriel was understanding and more than capable of filling in for now. There was money in the budget to hire other designers on an as-needed, temporary basis if the workload became too heavy with existing staff. A twinge of guilt hit her as she hung up the phone, but she'd make it up to her assistant when everything returned to normal. Once all this was over, she'd offer Muriel a partnership in the firm.

The house smelled habitable again, if not peachy keen. Harper closed all the windows, sat at the kitchen table and went to work making a game plan on how to proceed with her quest. So far, the only motive she had for foul play was a boyfriend murderously unhappy about the pregnancy.

She drummed her pencil on the notebook but could think of no other lead to pursue. At least not for now. The unexplained noises and smell at home didn't concern her as much as the message to "get out of the house" and the truck that had barreled down on her by the mailbox. Sure, it was possible that both were random, unconnected incidents—but it was also possible that someone did not want her in Baysville. If that were the case, it had to be related to Presley. She had no conflict with anyone in this town.

Unease hammered her temples. From here on out, she'd have to be extra vigilant to ensure that all windows and doors stayed closed and tamperproof.

The lockdown began now.

"You've reached your destination. On right," the disembodied voice of the GPS announced.

Here? Liam frowned at the sight of an ugly cinderblock house that appeared to have been randomly dropped in the middle of a no-man's-land of marsh. Weeds grew up the sides of the moldy structure. A rusted Chevy truck was parked haphazardly on the side of the windowless building. At the back of the property stood an old barn, its rotten roof half collapsing in on the building. The place looked forlorn and neglected, as though no one lived within miles.

Unease lifted the tiny hairs on Liam's arms and the nape of his neck. It was way too quiet out here. Someone had anonymously reported a break-in at the house and left an address, but no name or phone number. Liam got on the two-way radio and reported his location and findings to the dispatcher.

"Want to wait on backup before approaching the house?" the dispatcher asked.

He hesitated. They were chronically short staffed, and it was close to quitting time for the first-shift crew. Already, the October sky had darkened. Only a few dying rays of sunlight cut through the gray clouds.

"No. The place appears deserted."

"Stay in radio contact," the dispatcher advised.

"Ten-four." Liam pulled the cruiser near the front door and shut off the engine before easing out. The quiet was deafening, a heavy pressure that rang in his ears. A flock of starlings abruptly flew out of a sweetgum tree, their collective wings flapping as noisily and erratically as his heartbeat. The birds made their way skyward, still in search of the perfect night's roosting spot.

Cautiously, Liam approached the house and knocked at the door. Complete silence greeted his overture; not even the whisper of movement could be detected from within. He knocked again. "Anyone home?" he called out. "It's the police."

Nothing. Liam backed away and peered into the first front window. Through a thick layer of dust, he made out a single cot surrounded by trash. Did anyone even live in this place? At the second front window, he observed a small room that held an old couch that had stuffing bursting out of threadbare upholstery and more trash scattered on old carpeting. He made his way to the back of the house, which only had one door and window. Again, he looked through the window into a tiny kitchen, where dirty pots and pans overflowed from a sink, and more trash, mostly empty fast food containers, littered the counter and floor.

There wasn't anything even worth stealing from this place. If anyone had wanted in, it would be merely to seek temporary shelter from the coming night. Liam glanced over his shoulder at the decrepit old barn. Might as well search it to be thorough. He headed there then stopped, surprised to find a pattern of flattened weeds and grass. Someone had driven by recently. His gaze followed the tire tracks where they wound to the back of the barn.

This didn't feel right.

Might be best to return to his vehicle and drive around back to check out the area. Liam switched on the two-way. "Nobody found at the residence," he reported. "But I'm—"

A loud pop cracked, and a whizzing torpedoed

the air, invisible and swift. A crushing swath of fire radiated from the side of his left leg.

"Officer Andrews? Are you all right?"

On instinct, he dropped to the ground on his belly and withdrew his sidearm, flicking off the safety. The cold ground rumbled beneath him at the same moment he heard rustling from the barn. A large figure, clad all in black and wearing a knitted black ski cap, burst from the barn and ran, headed to a copse of pines not twenty feet away.

"Halt," he ordered. "Police!"

"Officer Andrews?" The dispatcher's voice came again. "An officer possibly down!" she cried out, quickly calling out the address.

The man kept running. Liam shot into the air— but the fleeing felon never even slowed. Damn it. The man had a getaway vehicle or another driver waiting that was parked nearby and out of sight. Warm dampness spread down his left leg, and he noted the scent of blood. Liam pushed down the injury aftereffects; he'd deal with that later. For now, he needed to seek cover in case his pursuer took another shot. He struggled to his feet, wincing as his left leg crumpled at the slightest weight. The twenty feet to the barn felt like a mile as he limped to shelter. From a distance, an engine came to life. Through the barn slats, he witnessed low, narrow beams of light heading in the opposite direction of the main road. His shooter was escaping in a four-wheeler.

"Officer Andrews?"

He raised the walkie-talkie to his mouth. "Here,"

he responded breathily, surprised at the effort required to speak. Now the danger had passed, his adrenaline bottomed out and pain registered through his former numbing shock. He stretched his leg, wincing at the stabbing agony. The vortex of pain was localized about three inches above his left knee on the outer side. Luckily for him, the bullet hadn't landed a smidge farther right and shattered his kneecap. But that didn't mean he was by any means grateful for the burning bullet now lodged under his skin.

A siren sounded. It felt odd to realize it was his own signal that help would shortly arrive. Usually, he was the man responding to other people's emergencies. Grimacing, he again stood and painstakingly made his way out of the barn, fighting back a sudden wave of nausea and dizziness.

He recognized Sam as his fellow officer exited the cruiser and ran toward him. *His fellow officer.* Running to help him despite any threats of danger. What would Sam and the others think if they knew the real reason he was in Baysville? Would they view him as a traitor?

And what if that bullet had been meant as more than a mere warning—if the shooter had aimed at his heart?

Chapter Seven

Harper threw her car keys on the counter and picked up a note from Kimber. The cleaning crew she had recommended would arrive tomorrow morning. At least that was something. Today's library research had been a bust. Surprisingly little had been written on Presley's death.

She headed upstairs, sipping a glass of wine. On her bed, she hit the remote button to turn on the TV and rubbed her eyes, still bleary from viewing internet articles and microfiche documents. Lethargy set in and the dark abyss of sleep beckoned. And yet, her mind resisted the vulnerability of sleep.

Something about this house was all wrong. She could deny it all she liked during the day with her rational brain, but here, alone at night, fear insinuated itself like a chilling fog rolling over her in waves. Here, her childhood home held no charm or happiness. No comforting memories of love. No cheery reminiscences to indulge in. Instead, it contained pain and loss and sorrow. Even more, the house oozed a sentient, living vibe, as though the very walls were listening to her every breath. Watching her every move. Possessing an unknown menace that could pounce upon her at any moment.

Just as it had done to Presley.

All wrong, all wrong... The warning refrain echoed through her. But her weary body accepted the peace and promise of rest. Just a few minutes to recharge. What could it hurt?

Skreek.

Worry clawed at the back of her sleeping mind, a frantic warning that all was not right.

Skreek. Skreek.

An explosion of noise erupted close by, and she awoke in a flash of panic. There was no disorientation or gradual floating back to consciousness. One second she'd been dead to the world, lost in a cocoon of oblivion, and then the next second she sat straight up, clutching a pillow. The small TV set on the dresser gave off an artificial glow that cast deep shadows in the bedroom. A reporter's monotone voice sounded over video footage of a riot somewhere in a country far away. Maybe the noise had merely been gunfire from the TV news broadcast.

She willed her mind to accept the rational explanation. What else could it have possibly been? Yet her heart rate barely slowed its frantic pace.

The sound came again. *Bam bam bam bam bam...* A dozen mini bombs detonating in rapid succession, followed closely by loud rolling swishes—as though a bag of marbles had been upended onto the hardwood floor.

What the hell? Her heart pounded as though trying to break free of her rib cage.

Heavy breathing pervaded the air. A menacing pant—slow, deep, deliberate.

She couldn't move. Arms and legs stiffened into paralysis. There was only the rapid rise and fall of her chest.

A cackle broke out, witchy and guttural.

Her tongue lay thick and heavy in her dry mouth; she couldn't have answered even if she'd wanted to.

This couldn't be happening. She glanced at the nearly empty glass of wine on the nightstand. The alcohol, perhaps? But no, it had never affected her this way before.

The breathy voice chuckled with a tinny echo. It held no familiarity to her ears. A whimper escaped past her numb lips, and she scooted backward, her spine pressed into the wooden headboard.

The eternal scratching started up, like a mischief of mice. "Go away," she cried, flinging a book against the wall.

Don't you love me, Harper? You're my sister. My baby sister.

She should run, get the hell out of the house and never come back. Unexpected silence descended, and she tensed, waiting for the next round. Because it always came back. Every. Damn. Time.

The tinkling of shattered glass erupted, followed by a sniveling, as though a person was crying.

There was a knock—a sharp rap that sounded

loud enough to splinter wood. Harper clamped her hands over her ears.

"Get out of here! You aren't real. You can't be." She was officially losing her mind now, talking to a make-believe person in her head.

All sound ceased, but the threat lingered in the darkness. A promise. A harbinger of doom. It would come back again one night. Harper was sure of it.

She'd come home to get answers. And if the answer was that she was crazy, then she'd have to accept that and get counseling. Harper waited, hardly daring to breathe, in case the noises returned.

They didn't. Not this time. Maybe it had been her imagination, after all. Maybe she was oversensitive to normal sounds old houses made.

She turned up the volume on the TV and downed what was left in her wineglass. There'd be no more sleep tonight. For a distraction, she changed the channel to watch the late-night news. It held little interest—until the announcement that a local police officer had been shot.

Harper gasped and leaned forward at the video of EMTs pushing a stretcher into an ambulance. The injured officer was strapped down, but she caught a glimpse of sandy-colored hair.

Liam.

Her heart pinched at the brief glimpse of his pale face. How badly was he hurt? What if… She couldn't bear to think of it. Liam would recover. He'd been conscious as the camera had panned over his body. A good sign.

Liam hadn't been in Baysville too long, and she knew for a fact that his relationship with Bryce was strained. The other times she'd observed him with his fellow cops, it seemed as though there was a reserve in their interactions.

Her instinct was to rush down to the hospital, to be a friend.

The least she could do was pay him a visit and offer to sit with him until family or a friend arrived. She'd rather be in a bleak hospital room all night than tossing and turning in bed.

Decision made, Harper strode to the mirror and ran a hand through her tousled hair. With only a moment's hesitation, she left her bedroom and went to the bathroom, splashing her face with cold water. She reached for the towel, but her hand grasped air. What the hell? Had it dropped on the floor? Mystified, she glanced around and then shrugged. Must have thrown it in the wash and forgotten to replace it with a clean one. Ablutions completed, Harper flipped on all the lights as she made her way downstairs.

STARK LIGHTS, UNFAMILIAR voices and an antiseptic chill in the air sent goose bumps down his arms. Liam narrowed his eyes and caught sight of a man in white, a stethoscope dangling from his neck. That's right—he was in the hospital. Evidently, he'd lost consciousness for a bit. A blessing considering the pain radiating like a heat wave from his left leg.

"We've removed the bullet," a doctor assured him, leaning over the hospital bed. "You're going to be fine. Might be a bit sore for a few days, though. Best if you stay off your feet. We're going to give you a numbing shot and send you home with a prescription for pain pills."

The sharp jab of a needle punctured the wound's tender flesh, immediately followed by a blessed cooling. A nurse wheeled him out of recovery and to a temporary room for a couple more hours of observation. No sooner had he transferred from the wheelchair to a cot than Bryce entered the room, deep worry lines etched in his broad forehead.

"Damn, Andrews," he said, running a hand through his dark hair. "Looks like you had a close call tonight."

"Not really."

"Looks that way to me. I talked to my men who arrived at the scene and got your statement."

The nurse interrupted, pointing to the metal drawer beside the cot. "Your clothes are in there. Let me know if you need help getting into them. Once you're dressed, we'll see about sending you home. Although, like the doctor told you, it would be best if you remained overnight."

"Thanks, but I insist on being discharged. I can manage on my own," he assured her before turning to Bryce. "If the shooter had meant to kill me, he had ample opportunity. This shot was a warning."

Skepticism flashed across his features. "A warning? About what?"

"Don't know yet." Liam scooted off the bed, placing all his weight on his right leg and testing the left.

Even with the numbing shot, it tingled. He sat back down and withdrew a plastic bag of bloody clothing from the nightstand. No way he was putting those on.

Bryce lifted the bag he held in his hands. "Take this. A new uniform. Figured the old one would be shredded."

"Thanks, man. I'll take my badge off my old shirt and throw the old uniform in the trash."

"Let's get back to what you said about the shooting being a warning," Bryce said. "You probably just caught a robber unawares. Plain bad luck."

"Doubt that old house had anything worth stealing. Couple that with the anonymous phone tip, and I'd say that shooter was waiting on me."

"The dispatcher traced the call, but—"

"Let me guess. It was to a throwaway phone." Liam untied his hospital gown and donned the new uniform shirt.

His boss nodded as he buttoned his shirt. "Even more reason to suspect it was a warning." Bryce scraped his face with a broad palm. "Not a very good warning if you don't know what it is you're supposed to be warned away from. You got any ideas?"

Did he ever. But Bryce was the last person he'd confide in. Liam observed him closely as he cautiously pulled up the new uniform pants, careful to avoid touching the bandaged wound, taking his time as he adjusted to the twinges of pain. His boss looked like hell, as though he'd been too long without sleep and stressed to the max. Had Bryce discovered what his newest employee was up to? Had his cover been blown? "Not a clue," Liam deadpanned. "What about you? You got any theories?"

"Can't help wondering if it somehow relates to Harper Catlett. Trouble seems to follow that family."

"Why? Because her sister died in an accidental fire?"

Bryce winced but doggedly continued with his theory. "The minute she returns to town and starts asking questions, look what happens. She drew you in with her claims about a possible stalker and now this. We've never had an officer shot in Baysville before."

"Coincidence," Liam insisted. If he played it smart, he'd let Bryce continue with his delusion. Keeping his boss focused on the wrong path could only help Liam preserve his cover. But he hated Harper being wrongfully suspected of anything to do with tonight's incident.

"I don't believe in coincidences."

"Why are you suddenly turning on Harper, linking her to this? You made it clear from the start that you believed her fear was all in her head. That her sister's death was an accident and anything strange happening in the house was only her imagination."

"Call it intuition."

"You don't believe in coincidences? Well, I don't believe in intuition." With that, Liam zipped his pants and then sat on the bed as he slipped into his old, muddied uniform shoes, hiding his pain as he bent to pull them on.

Bryce quirked a brow. "You've never had a gut feeling on the job?"

"Sure. But what people often call a gut feeling is actually based on fact. Like last night, I had a feeling something was wrong when I was merely picking up on environmental clues that I too quickly discounted—the isolated location, the anonymous call, the subconscious awareness that somebody was watching me."

"Semantics. You're quibbling, Andrews. Harper's bad news. I tried to warn you."

Liam shrugged. Either Bryce was too dense to understand his illogical distrust, or—worst-case scenario—Bryce had found out about the undercover investigation and was taking aggressive measures to scare him off track. Either way, Liam had never quit an assignment, and he wasn't about to start now. Whatever it took, he'd get to the bottom of the vagrant murders and discover if the Baysville PD were involved in some sort of cover-up.

"Can I give you a lift home?" Bryce asked.

"If it's not too much trouble, then—"

They both turned at the sound of a light knock on the semiclosed door. "May I come in?"

A bolt of warmth shot through his gut at the familiar voice. Before he could answer, Harper's head peeked around the door.

Bryce sighed and strode across the room. "I suspect you'd rather ride home with Harper than me. Take as much time off as you need to recover, Andrews," he called over his shoulder. He nodded at Harper and quickly exited the room.

Harper strolled over, her red hair practically ablaze under the merciless fluorescent lights. He wanted nothing more than to brush his face against its sweet warmth and run his hands through the silken fire. After his abrupt rejection the previous night, Liam couldn't have been more startled at her appearance. Or more grateful.

"I heard what happened on the news. Hope you don't mind me dropping in." Her eyes slowly scanned his body from head to toe. "Are you okay?"

"I'm fine. Just a flesh wound. They've already dug out the bullet and stitched me up."

Her lips trembled. She reached out a hand as though to touch him, then thought better of it and dropped it down by her side. "Bryce said you could use a ride home?"

Damn, he hated not being able to drive himself. Being dependent on anyone made him nuts. "Looks that way. But if you'd rather not, I'll call a cab or an Uber."

"At this time of night? Not happening in this town."

"Right."

They regarded one another awkwardly. As for himself, Liam recalled lying in the marsh, bleeding, in pain and waiting for backup—and all he could think about was Harper.

"When this is over," he began slowly, "if you're still in town, then maybe…" His voice trailed off.

"Maybe," she breathed. Harper ran her fingers lightly down his face, and he closed his eyes, marveling at the soft caress that made his entire body heat. His whole adult life he'd been an outsider, always on the outskirts of intimacy and true friendship. Because of his undercover work, everyone was either a suspect or not to be trusted in keeping his secret.

But Harper felt like home after a long trip. When this case was over...

"Excuse me. Looks like you're ready to check out," a nurse said, entering the room.

Harper dropped her hand and stepped away. The nurse practically winked. "Let's get your paperwork in order and you can go home."

Home with Harper. Suddenly, the night didn't seem all bad.

Chapter Eight

She hurried into the hallway, eager to pull her car around front to the hospital's main entrance. Liam should be signed out and waiting by then. The two nurses on night duty didn't even glance up from their charts as she walked by. On each side of her, most of the patient room doors were ajar. Machines beeped and hummed, emitting an industrial green glow punctuated by the flashing of red buttons. People lay quiet, attached to IVs and tubes. Thank goodness Liam hadn't been severely injured and facing a prolonged stay.

Her sneakers scrunched on the polished linoleum and echoed through the labyrinth of hallways, a stick-slip squeak of rubber.

Another set of rubber-soled shoes chirped from behind. She stopped and swiftly turned, hoping it wasn't a nurse unexpectedly canceling Liam's discharge orders.

The hall stood empty, save for an open patient door that swayed slightly, as though recently entered. Her throat tightened. *Probably just a nurse dispens-*

ing medication. Harper continued to the elevators and punched the ground-floor button, quickly getting on when it arrived almost immediately. As it lowered, she exhaled a sigh, glad to be on her way. She exited and made her way through the now-empty lobby.

Squeak, squeak.

The mystery person was back. He must have taken the stairs when she'd opted for the elevator. Discreetly, Harper slightly turned her head, but she only caught a glimpse of a tall person in a white coat as he whisked by a coffee kiosk. Absolutely no reason for the sensation of spiders skittering down her spine. She frowned, noting the absence of blue-uniformed cops hanging around the entrance door. They'd probably all migrated to the ER section, where any action would be taking place.

To top it off, a storm had arrived. Trees swayed in the wet gusts and the clatter of rain on the roof and pavement intensified several decibels. Of course, she'd left home in a hurry with no umbrella. Nothing for it but to brave the elements. Harper rushed into the night. By the time she'd crossed the street, her clothes were drenched and her hair plastered to her cheeks and neck.

Only a few vehicles remained in the concrete parking deck. She spotted hers right away and dug out the keys from her purse.

There was no inexplicable warning sound, only the mechanical hum of the overhead lights, but Harper knew the instant she was no longer alone.

Probably another visitor like herself, but she quickened her pace and clicked the remote to open her car door. The responding beep of her vehicle in the parking deck echoed, loud and jarring, accompanied by the explosive flash of her headlights.

Harper got in the car and locked it before starting the engine. *See, you're fine.* Nearby, another car engine sounded, but no headlights flashed on. She hit the gas and exited, relieved to leave the gloomy concrete lot. Liam waited at the door with a nurse when she pulled up to the entrance.

"Take good care of him," the nurse said, waving goodbye.

Liam eased into the seat, a wince creasing his face.

"I hope they gave you some pain pills in case you need them before the pharmacy opens."

He held up a plastic bag. "They're in here, though I don't plan to take one."

She drove away and followed his directions, on past the outskirts of town, leaving behind the quiet, deserted streets for a country road without streetlamps. Inky darkness pervaded while sheets of rain slashed at the windows.

"Another mile before we get to my place," Liam said. "Sorry you have to drive in such bad weather."

Headlights suddenly flashed from behind, drawing closer and closer. As though rushing forward to consume them. She pressed her foot on the gas pedal. Liam turned in the seat, frowning.

"They're going way too fast and getting way too close. Especially on these wet roads."

"Too bad we aren't in your cruiser. Bet if we turned on the blue lights they'd back off in a hurry."

Harper lifted her chin to peer at the rearview mirror. Through the pounding rain, she was able to make out the vehicle's outline.

"Oh, great, not again," she muttered. "A black pickup truck." Not her favorite after nearly being run down by one on her own front lawn.

An explosive sound rang out. "That wasn't thunder, was it?" she asked.

"Hell, no. They took a shot at us." Liam reached for his right pocket, then swore. "Bryce took my sidearm at the hospital for safekeeping."

Harper's heart beat painfully as she floored the accelerator. The tires squealed, and the vehicle swayed from side to side as she hydroplaned. *Stay calm.* She eased her foot off the gas and steered it back to the right side of the road.

Liam called for emergency assistance. But by the time help arrived, it would be too late. She had to do something, anything. *Think.* The truck started to pull up around her on the left. Its headlights were on bright and the beams blinding. Time for drastic measures. Less than an eighth of a mile ahead was a cutoff road. Again, she sped up and at the last possible second, turned the steering wheel sharply to the right.

"What the hell?" Liam braced his hands on the dashboard as her car skidded dangerously. But their pursuer was in an even worse predicament. The driver slammed on his brakes and the truck spun in circles.

Harper took a deep breath. Up ahead was another turn she could take and then reverse direction to head back in town. With any luck, the truck driver would either lose sight of them or he'd be reluctant to pursue them once they'd hit city limits.

"I think you've managed to lose him," Liam said, staring back at the truck. "Way to go. There's already an officer responding."

"Who are they after—you or me?"

"Maybe both of us."

From a distance, sirens wailed. Harper turned on a side street.

"Damn. He's getting away." Liam returned to the dispatcher on the phone and reported that the truck was speeding north on County Road 78.

"Think they'll catch up to him?" she asked.

"Doubtful." Liam eyed her appreciatively. "Smart thinking back there. Probably saved our lives."

"Now what? Shall I drive to the police station?" They were back in Baysville, and her tight grip on the steering wheel relaxed.

"Pull over a minute." He held up a finger, listening to the dispatcher. Harper stopped the car by the side of the road and watched his face for long minutes.

"Thanks. Not a bad idea. See you in the morning." Liam punched a button and laid the phone down.

"Well?"

"The truck was long gone by the time they arrived. Bryce is sending an officer to periodically drive by my house all evening, just to be safe. I think you'd be safer staying with me tonight than driving home and being alone."

"Can't say I relish the idea of being alone, either."

Harper pulled back onto the road and drove to Liam's, keeping a wary eye out for another round with their mysterious truck driver. By the time they arrived at his home and got out of the car, her knees were unsteady, and exhaustion had set in. They made a dash through the rain and then Liam unlocked the door.

She entered his neat, well-kept ranch house. Leather furniture, a large-screen TV, wooden coffee and end tables—it all screamed Standard Bachelor Decor. No knickknacks, artwork, pillows or froufrou of any kind graced the masculine abode. Which was fine—minimalism was a statement of its own, and as an interior designer she could appreciate the style. Yet it lacked a personal touch.

"You're renting this place, I take it?" she asked.

He hobbled over to the couch, eschewing her outstretched arm offering support. "How'd you guess?"

"Nothing on the walls. No photos anywhere." Or books or anything else to indicate his tastes or family life. "Can I fix you something to drink?"

"I'd say a beer, but I imagine that's off-limits with the meds they plied into me at the hospital. Water, please."

She found a water bottle in the fridge and returned to the den. His face was pale, and fine lines pinched the corners of his eyes and lips. He was obviously still in some pain, whether or not he wanted to admit it. Pinpricks of guilt assaulted her. She couldn't shake wondering if her poking into Presley's death had anything to do with everything that had happened tonight. "Need anything else?" she asked, handing him the bottled water.

"I'm good. Thank you…for everything."

He took a long swig while she fidgeted with the cuffs of her sweater. "Do you think the shooting and tonight's chase had anything to do with you helping me look into Presley's death?"

Liam slowly lowered the bottle and shook his head. "Don't see how."

"Maybe Allen…" She let the suggestion slip unsaid into the gulf between them.

"Spencer might be a creep and scumbag, but a rogue shooter? He's too much of a coward. I don't see it."

"He could have hired someone to do the dirty work," she insisted.

"I don't believe he's that creative or has those connections, but I can have another talk with him."

She nodded and took a look around. "So do you have a spare bedroom? If not, I can sleep on the sofa. It's only a few hours until dawn, anyway. If you need me for any reason, I'll be here."

"Your idea has one serious flaw."

"What's that?"

"We should stay in the same bed." He quickly held up a hand. "I'm not saying we should have sex." Liam's voice dropped to a deep, gruff tone. "Although if you want to…"

A smile crooked one side of his mouth.

It shot through her like lightning, then relief—and a tad of disappointment—whooshed out of her lungs, and she gave a shaky laugh.

"Seriously, though, after all these potshots at us, I'd sleep better where I can keep an eye on you." Liam rose to his feet, still careful to keep most of his weight on his right leg.

Heavy static suddenly crackled through the den, and she spun, searching for the source.

"It's okay, I've got a police scanner and a two-way radio," he explained, pointing to the maze of boxes and wires on top of a table on the far side of the room. "Even an old-fashioned landline phone and an answering machine."

Disembodied voices talked in some kind of cop code about an incident three streets over. She gathered that a citizen had called in complaining of a strange person creeping through their backyard.

"Must be the Shadow Dweller," she said with a tired smile.

He groaned. "Not you, too. Any time property goes missing or someone's roaming where they shouldn't, y'all are quick to blame it on this mysterious Shadow Dweller."

"He's a local legend." She walked to the scanner, her hand hovering over the power button. "Don't you want me to turn this thing off? Listening to it is above and beyond the call of duty. Especially when you're supposed to be resting."

"Leave it. I like to keep a pulse on what's happening, in case I might be needed. That's why I even keep the landline as a backup to my cell. Never know when something big might break."

"What kind of things go on in our small town?" she asked curiously.

"You'd be surprised. Besides the homeless men killings, there's plenty of talk about a gambling and prostitution ring, not that I've been able to verify it."

"Here in Baysville? I've never caught wind of that kind of activity."

Liam hobbled across the den and into the hallway. "It's kept on the down low." He glanced into the kitchen. "Hungry?"

"I'm good. Want me to fix you anything?"

"Nah."

She followed him into a clean, though stark, bedroom with dark wood furniture and utilitarian blinds over the lone window. The bed loomed before her, and again her face flushed with heat. Liam sat on the edge of the mattress, kicked off his shoes and patted the empty space beside him. "Come here."

Self-consciously, Harper kicked off her shoes as well and eased onto the bed beside him.

"I want you to feel safe, and I want to know you're safe. You can sleep here on the bed. I'll lay a few blankets down and sleep on the floor."

The thought of him, with his injuries, sleeping on the hard floor, appalled her. "No, you won't!" she said forcefully, and then wondered if she was sending the wrong message. "I'll take the floor if you'd rather not share the bed."

"It's not that I don't want to share. I want you to be comfortable."

"I am comfortable. I trust you."

His fingers interlaced with hers, and they lay together staring into the darkness, a falling rain pattering on the roof like a lullaby. The warmth of his body beside her was both comforting and intimate. So much nicer than tossing and turning in her own bed at home, waiting to hear unexplained scratchings and whispers that defied rational explanation. His fingers lightly traced a pattern, circling up from her palms and then the inside of her forearms up to her elbows. She'd never considered that an erogenous zone, but everywhere Liam touched her leaped to an awakening of her senses.

"You must be exhausted," she finally commented.

"A little, but also a bit wound up. Talk to me awhile if you're not too tired. Tell me more about your family."

"It's too sad. They're all gone. I'd rather hear about yours. What are your parents and siblings like?"

A tired grin ghosted across his wan face. "Noisy. Full of energy. Growing up with three brothers and two sisters, plus all of their friends that hung out at our place, there was always something going on."

It sounded wonderful to her. The Catlett home had been much too quiet after Dad and Presley's deaths.

The kind of heavy silence that weighed on a person's mind and soul, a dreadful emptiness that hammered at the heart from the absence of loved ones. "What about that Uncle Teddy of yours you mentioned? Is he the reason you're so kind to the homeless men that hang out by the railroad tracks?"

"I don't do that much for the men," he protested. "Just take them out some food and clothing from time to time. I'd like to think that someone did the same for my uncle when he passed through here."

She rolled on her side and regarded him in surprise. "How do you know he was ever in Baysville?"

"He'd been arrested a couple times for holing up in vacant buildings. Even spent a few days in the local jail."

"That's so sad."

"Let's not talk about sad stuff tonight," Liam said softly, gently squeezing her fingers. "Thank you for being here."

For a few moments, they rested in silence, but she could tell he couldn't sleep, and neither could she. There was a connection between them, something beyond the case of her sister's death, the homeless man's murder and Liam's shooting. She genuinely cared for him. She wanted to be closer to him, and after the events of the past few days, she wasn't in a mood to wait.

She kissed him full on the lips, conscious of the heat of his body, the woodsy scent of him. Her core tightened with hunger, and she moaned in protest when he broke the kiss.

"I promised to keep my hands to myself," he explained gruffly.

Maybe I don't want you to. But she bit back the words and squeezed his hand. The poor guy had just taken a bullet to his leg tonight and was pumped up with pain meds. He needed rest.

Harper settled into a peaceful lull as Liam slowly drifted to sleep, listening to his slowed breath, her hand resting on the rise and swell of his chest. The *rightness* of this moment couldn't be denied. Liam had come into her life for a reason, she was certain of it, even if the timing was all wrong.

Liam made her feel as though no obstacles were too difficult to face. A resurgence of optimism made her lips tug into a smile. Quietly, she eased off the bed and tiptoed into the hallway. A small glass of water, a trip to the bathroom, and then she'd lie back down beside Liam and—hopefully—fall into untroubled sleep.

"Andrews, you there?" The deep, male voice cut through the quiet house—abrupt and demanding. "It's Eason. Pick up the phone. We need to discuss the next gambling game and arrange a meeting with the women."

Harper pulled up short. Gambling? Women—as in *hookers*? What did Liam have to do with any of this?

Mattress springs squeaked, followed by heavy footsteps pounding the floor. Liam raced past her, surprisingly fast considering his injury, and grabbed the phone in the den. "Eason? Why are you calling me on this line?" A short pause and then, "No. Not yet. I need more time. Obviously, I've made progress. If you come now, it'll ruin everything." Another pause. "Yeah, yeah. I'm fine, no problem."

Liam hung up the phone and slowly turned to face her. The blue glow from all the equipment on the table cast an unnatural pallor on his harsh features. She didn't know this man like she thought she did. *He's not who he says he is.* What else didn't she know about him? And to think she'd been so content moments ago. Harper swallowed past the knot in her throat.

"Who are you?" she whispered.

BLOODY HELL. JUST WHEN they'd reestablished trust. But it was his own damn fault. He'd forgotten to take his cell phone to the bedroom. Naturally, Eason was worried once he'd gotten wind of the shooting and there'd been no response to his text messages. He'd been much too distracted from his usual routine by a combination of sedatives and a certain beautiful redhead—who now stared at him with a wide-eyed skepticism.

He approached slowly, palms held open at his sides. "I don't suppose there's any chance you could just forget what you overheard?"

"Not a chance."

He sighed. "Didn't think so."

Her eyes darted past him, to her purse lying on top of the coffee table. Was she actually afraid of him and wanting to make a quick getaway? There was no hope for it. He had to come clean. *Even if it means blowing your cover? Sacrificing all these months of work?* He could practically hear Eason's outraged words at what he was about to disclose.

"What's going on?" She took a step back, eyes narrowed.

The easiest way out of this mess was to show her. Liam walked forward, and she backed against the wall, avoiding his touch. "I'm going to get my wallet out of my pants pocket," he explained.

He strode past her and flipped on the bedroom lights, picked his pants up off the floor and retrieved his wallet. He turned, relieved to find that Harper stood in the doorway—he'd half expected her to grab her purse and run. Liam pulled a badge from his wallet and handed it to her. "I'm working undercover for the Virginia ATF field division.

"ATF?" she asked, squinting at the badge.

"Bureau of Alcohol, Tobacco and Firearms."

She handed him back the badge. "What's that got to do with gambling and prostitution?"

"The name doesn't fully encompass our range of authority. We also investigate any threat to public safety from organized crime."

"Really?" Her lips twisted, and she placed her hands on her hips. "Seems like your bureau could have chosen more likely towns than ours to infiltrate. We must be small potatoes compared to larger cities."

"But not all towns have a string of unsolved murders like Baysville."

"The homeless killings?"

"We have reason to believe the killer, or killers, are involved in an organized crime ring related to gambling and prostitution."

"The mafia? Here?" Her voice rose in disbelief.

"Not on that kind of scale." Her blue-gray eyes regarded him with a mixture of hope and wariness. How far was he willing to explain his undercover discoveries without knowing if she'd even believe his story?

"The crimes in Baysville are localized, without ties to a larger crime ring," he hedged.

She tapped an index finger against her lips, considering his words. "Tonight's shooting was no random robbery gone bad. And someone was after you on the drive home as well. You're getting too close to the truth. Which is making someone very nervous."

Relief melted the twisted knots in his shoulders. Harper understood. "Exactly. It was a warning."

"But who…" She paused, studying his set face. "You can't tell me. Probably not a good idea for me to know anyway."

"Knowledge can be dangerous."

The numbing injection at the wound site was wearing off, replaced by an itchy burning. Standing around arguing all night wasn't what the doctor ordered. He ran a hand through his hair, silently giving in to the weariness.

"You need to rest," she said, taking him by the elbow and guiding him back to bed.

HE SETTLED INTO the warm cotton covers. Again, he sought her hand, and their fingers interlaced. Heaven help him, he could get used to this. To Harper's sweet body beside him, making love to her every night and waking with her in his arms every morning. Dangerous, forbidden longings. Lethargy overcame his whirling thoughts, and yet one more thing needed saying aloud.

"Thank you again," he murmured.

"It's the least I could do after you believed in me when I reported that email threat. And for not believing Bryce when he hinted I was mentally unstable. Even if…well, never mind about that."

He was wide-awake now. Liam switched on the bedside lamp and leaned on an elbow, staring down into her troubled eyes. "Never mind about what?"

"Shouldn't have opened my big mouth. You're not the type to let something go."

"So tell me then."

She sighed and ran a hand through her red tresses that pooled on the white pillowcase. "There've been more strange noises at the house. It seems to be getting worse."

Liam sucked in his breath. "There has to be a logical explanation. There's no such thing as ghosts."

"That's what I used to think." She laughed without mirth. "Either my house is haunted, or everyone is right about me. I'm a basket case."

He smoothed a lock of hair from her cheek and tucked it behind her ear. "I reject both those posits."

"Then how do you account for the weird noises?"

"I don't know," he admitted. "But we'll figure it out. Together."

Chapter Nine

Daytime is safe.

Liam had insisted on going in to work today, hoping to get a lead on the possible owner of the truck that had chased them last night, and she had her own agenda of things to do. Harper sprinted up the steps to her house.

She felt herself grin, remembering her awakening next to Liam. If she'd thought their first kiss had been spectacular, it was child's play compared to this morning's toe-curling kiss. She bounded inside, 100 percent more lighthearted than when she'd left.

First things first. Harper entered the basement and gasped at the change. Kimber's crew had done amazing work. Every shelf, tool and box was gone, just as she'd requested. They'd even swept the floors and washed the high windows. Worth every damn penny. She promptly called her friend and invited her over for coffee. Just mailing a check seemed too impersonal.

Harper proceeded upstairs and into Mom's room. Today, she'd take all those packed-up boxes to Goodwill and check off another section of the house as completed. After more than a dozen trips up and down the stairs, Harper loaded up her car and then headed to the kitchen to start the coffee. The aroma of fresh-ground beans revived her flagging energy, and she happily pulled cups and saucers from the cupboards. There was a pack of chocolate chip cookies, not homemade but they would have to do. Kimber wouldn't take but a couple of nibbles anyway.

Tires crunched gravel, and she glanced out the window to spot Kimber emerging from her Town Car. She wore an expensive-looking navy pantsuit and the same tight, worried expression Harper had witnessed at their last meeting. What had happened to the bright-eyed, happy cheerleader from high school? Now she thought about it, Kimber's temperamental descent had been gradual over the last few years. At first, Harper had attributed it to stress from building her real estate career and managing a large family. Now, she wasn't so sure. Marital problems, perhaps? She and Richard always seemed so perfect for one another, so in love. But no one could ever know what went on with a couple behind closed doors.

Harper threw open the front door with a welcoming smile, determined to cheer up Kimber. "Hey there, come on in." She gave her a hug, holding it for an extra second before ushering her to the kitchen table. "You sit down and relax while I fix you a cup."

"I can't stay long, I have an open house in less than an hour." Instead of sitting, Kimber walked down the hallway, peering in rooms. "Looks like you've made progress clearing out the place."

"A room a day. That's the game plan."

"So, by that rate, I take it you'll be finished here within the week." She returned to the kitchen and perched on the edge of a chair. A ball of nervous energy always ready to take flight.

"More or less." Harper set their drinks on the table.

"Have you thought any more about my offer?"

"I'm staying put for the time being. If I decide to sell later, I'll let you know."

Kimber's eyes flashed. "What do you mean? Don't you need to get back to your job in Atlanta?"

The sharp edge in Kimber's voice caught her unawares, and she sipped her drink to consider her next words.

"I've made arrangements, so everything's covered in my absence." Harper slid a check across the table. "Thanks for your help. I included a little extra money so you can tip all the workers."

Kimber stuffed the check in her designer purse, then sipped her coffee, her face pensive.

"Is everything all right, Kimber? I mean, you don't have to tell me the specifics if you don't want to, but you seem a bit wound up. I'm concerned about you."

"Me?" She set down her cup with a decided thud, her brows drawn together. "I'm perfectly fine. Why would anything be wrong?"

And yet, Kimber's smile was brittle, and that sharp edge remained in her tone.

Harper regarded her somberly. Kimber had never been one to confide if she were having problems. She liked everyone to think her life was perfect, that she could handle anything on her own.

"I'm not trying to pry into your business," she said gently. "It just appears to me like—oh, I don't know—like you don't have any joy in your life lately. You're always busy or stressed."

Kimber sat up straighter, bristling with indignation. "I own my own business. Of course I'm busy. And you of all people should know how stressful that can be. Plus, I have a family and you…"

"Don't," she supplied drily.

To Harper's surprise, Kimber's eyes filled with tears.

Harper grabbed a tissue and handed it to Kimber. "We've been friends a long time. You've seen me at my worst and took me under your wing from middle school on up. I'll never forget that. So if there's a problem and you want to talk, I'm always here."

Kimber blew her nose and sniffled. "It's nothing. Just stress from trying to keep up with everything. Teenagers. A business."

Harper nodded sympathetically and waited for her friend to elaborate if she wanted.

But Kimber stood, clutching her purse like a lifeline. "Can't sit around all morning blubbering about my problems. Maybe one day next week you can come over to my place for a home-cooked meal. Richard will be glad to see you."

Harper doubted that. Richard was wrapped up in sports and motorcycles—two things she had no interest in. Not that she had anything against him or his hobbies—they just had nothing in common. And maybe she and Kimber didn't, either. Not anymore.

With a heavy heart, she walked her friend out to her car, where they exchanged perfunctory goodbyes before she returned to the house. Absentmindedly, she gazed out the window. A dreary pall fell over her spirits—until she thought of Liam and waking up in his arms. Harper straightened her shoulders. If he could go back to work this morning, she could do the same. From her research at the library, she'd garnered a list and phone numbers of Presley's old friends to call. Not that she planned on spreading the news of her sister's pregnancy, but she was curious if Presley might have confided in someone about her condition or problems she had with anyone.

Filled with renewed determination, she sat at the kitchen table and began making the calls. Over an hour later, Harper surveyed her dwindled list and notes. A couple of names had been scratched through as out of service, but most of Presley's old friends had been glad to reminisce about memories and old times. It cheered her that so many people remembered Presley with such fondness.

She tapped her pen on the table, trying to determine what action to take next. The old grandfather clock loudly ticked away the minutes, and she couldn't shake the feeling of impending doom. Maybe she and Liam could brainstorm later about the next course of action. With any luck, he'd have a few names of black-truck owners to investigate.

Decision made, Harper grabbed a container of shrimp scampi from the freezer and dumped it in a pan to heat up for lunch. This dish had been her sister's favorite. If Presley was still alive, the two of them could enjoy it together. Unexpected sadness pinched her heart.

A booming static infiltrated the quiet bustle of the kitchen. As if someone were in the next room and had switched on the TV or radio to an unclear channel. The fine hairs on her arm rose as she turned down the stove burner and nervously wiped her hands on her apron. She should go investigate. Yet her feet remained unmoving.

It stopped as suddenly as it had begun. She started to draw a relieved breath—*see? All is well*—when a stomp of slow, deliberate footsteps sounded from the basement.

She wasn't alone. Someone was in the house.

Harper stilled, struck by a frightening paralysis. The kind she experienced in dreams when danger approached and she couldn't run from an oncoming threat.

The basement door rattled. "Go away," she screamed, as though trying to reason with a ghost.

At last, her feet unglued from the tiled floor and she crossed over to the cabinet drawer that held the cutlery. She picked up the largest, sharpest knife available and gripped it tightly.

The stomping resumed, louder than before.

Harper crept across the dining room floor. A quick glance out the back window of the property revealed nothing out of the ordinary. She inched forward until she faced the closed basement door. Again, the stomping ceased as suddenly as it had begun.

What lay on the other side of the door?

Her need to know overcame her fear of the unknown. One quick, deep breath and Harper grabbed the doorknob with her left hand and jerked it open.

Cool, damp darkness awaited.

"Anybody down there?" she called out. *As if they would answer.* But the sound of her own voice was reassuring in itself.

Utter silence greeted her words.

Harper licked her dry lips and slowly stepped down the first three steps. Leaning forward, she surveyed the dark, still shadows. Thanks to the work of the cleaning crew, little remained in the basement. No place for anyone to hide. No explanation for the clomping footsteps.

She retraced her steps, careful not to turn her back on the darkness. Just in case. At the head of the stairwell, she shut the basement door, the sound of her own breathing loud and thick in the hushed house.

There had to be a rational explanation. Though not a one came to mind. In the meantime, she'd go to the hardware store and buy a lock. It might be useless and irrational, but it would help her sleep at night.

Harper returned to the kitchen and tossed the knife on the counter. The smell of burned butter had created a stench, so she turned off the stove and set the pan in the sink. Any desire to cook flew out the window. She wanted a break from being inside.

Air. She needed fresh air.

Harper went out the front door and into the yard, rubbing her arms. What the hell had just happened back there? It made no sense.

Mrs. Henley emerged from her cottage across the street, bundled in a sweater.

"Harper?" she called out. "What are you doing standing in the yard without a coat? It's cold out here."

The nip in the air had nothing to do with her body's involuntary shaking. Could she confide in Mrs. Henley?

"I, um, thought I heard something inside the house, and it freaked me out a little," she ventured.

Mrs. Henley shook her head in sympathy. "Your mom used to say she heard noises, too. But like I always used to tell Ruth, it's just the old house settling. Happens at my place all the time."

The news brought her up short. Mom heard weird stuff, too?

"Did Mom say what kind of noises?" she asked. "Or mention if she thought the place might be haunted?"

Faded blue eyes danced with mirth. "We used to

joke about it. I'd mention that Fred—my late husband—had been rattling around my house the previous night, making a general pest of himself. Then Ruth would tell me if she'd heard anything at her place. It was quite the joke between us."

Harper grabbed a fistful of the hair whipping about her face. Too bad she could find no humor in the joke.

Mrs. Henley laid a hand on her forearm. "Are you okay now?"

"I have an idea," she said, forcing joviality into her voice. "Would you like to come inside and keep me company while I make lunch? It would be a kindness."

As Harper suspected, her neighbor was delighted with the notion. She clasped her hands together at her chest. "Why, I'd love to. It'll be like old times with Ruth. We spent many an afternoon chatting over coffee. Why we'd talk up a storm about the latest books and TV shows and…"

Harper half tuned out the constant barrage of chatter. Had her mother humored the elderly widow by keeping her company, or had she really been lonely? Of course, she had been living all by herself. A guilty pang hammered her heart. She should have made an effort to visit more, to understand her mother better. Now it was too late.

They made their way to the front door, and even with Mrs. Henley by her side, Harper felt the familiar foreboding as she reentered the kitchen and turned on the stove. As her neighbor chattered away, Harper heated the shrimp scampi with unsteady hands, ears straining for any unexplained noises or whispers.

Of course, with a witness on hand, there wasn't a peep out of the resident ghost.

Chapter Ten

The sight always depressed him.

A cluster of dingy, sagging canvas tents and a few shelters that were nothing more than large strips of blue tarp hung between two trees. A huge campfire burned in the center of the vagrant gathering, and several men huddled over the warmth, the more fortunate holding sticks with hot dogs or other food scraps. The aroma was distinctive—burning oak mixed with roasted food and an unfortunate underlying note of rot. Empty tin cans, plastic jugs and other trash littered the outside edges of the tents. His mother would be dismayed to know that her brother had willingly chosen such a lifestyle, so Liam never filled her in on the finer details of the modern homeless living conditions.

He'd read reports estimating that over twenty thousand people chose this kind of fringe existence, but their numbers were dwindling and their culture drifting from the strict moral codes of the past. No one bemoaned this more than Gunner, who proudly claimed he'd jumped freight trains for decades traveling the country, although it was much harder now and at his age much too dangerous to continue.

As usual, Gunner was the first person to greet him. Liam limped over and waved.

"What happened to your leg?" Gunner shot a mostly toothless grin. "Did ya hurt yourself jumping the rails?"

"Not hardly. I don't have your physical agility," he joked, holding out the bag of groceries he'd brought with him.

The half a dozen other men scrambled to their feet and strode over, their faces pinched with cold and hunger. He knew all the regulars' names now, Sam, Grady, Biff, Tick and Buster. It'd taken Liam weeks to gain their trust so they'd accept his offerings of free food. Pride could be found in even the most humble of men.

Gunner doled out the provisions, equitably distributing the canned goods and other staples. The sandwich meat and bread he kept in the bag. "For supper tonight," he declared to the men before facing Liam again. "You need to speak with me?" he asked, lowering his voice.

"Yeah. Let's sit in my car a bit and warm up."

Once they were out of earshot of the others, Gunner cast him a worried frown. "So what happened to your leg?"

"Bullet wound. It's not as bad as it sounds. Just won't be suiting up for work a few days."

Gunner gave a low whistle but said nothing else

until they were safely ensconced in Liam's car. "Any of this related to what happened to Larry?"

"I feel sure of it. Proving that there's a correlation is another matter."

"We're starting to get scared. Baysville used to be a good resting spot, but now there's talk among the guys of moving on. Maybe heading farther south, at least for the winter."

"That's probably not a bad idea."

Gunner scrubbed at his lined, weathered face. "Don't feel like no place is safe no more," he admitted. "'Specially not at my age. The younger crowd that passes through here are rough. Drugs got 'em bad. No moral code. Ain't like the old days."

"Tell me about Larry. He one of the younger guys into drugs?"

"Nah, he seemed like a good dude. Always seemed to have a little cash on hand, although none of us knowed how he come by it. He'd disappear for hours and sometimes days, then show up with food and folding money."

"Dealing drugs, perhaps?"

"Not Larry. He had a son OD from drugs and was dead set against it."

"What about Ash, the guy killed last year? Did he spend time away from camp and return with cash?"

Gunner's eyes drifted upward and to the right as he cocked his head to one side. "I'll be damn. He sure did. Is there a connection, ya think?"

"I need to find out who they were working for.

Could be the key to unlocking the killer's identity. You have folks drop by here looking for work?"

"Sometimes. But work's more plentiful in the warmer seasons, when farmers are tending their fields or people need some painting done or some other odd job."

Liam thought it over carefully. He'd pieced together an illegal gambling operation that had recently begun expanding into prostitution. The homeless murders had to be tied in somehow—he just needed to figure out how. And for that, he needed Gunner.

"I suspect that with Larry's recent demise, someone else will approach one of you, offering cash in a shady business arrangement. Will you let me know if they do?"

"Sure thing, boss."

"I'll pay you for information."

"Ain't no need. We appreciate the groceries you bring out every week."

"I insist." He felt guilty enough involving Gunner in the mess. But whether or not Gunner turned informant, his life—and the other men's lives—were already in danger.

"Tell you what you can do," Gunner began, rubbing his scruffy chin.

"Name it."

"When this is over, help me find a job. A real job. Steady. Enough so's I can afford a proper shelter."

Liam regarded him with surprise. "You're giving up the life?"

"Case ya haven't noticed, I'm getting old." Gunner cackled and straightened his tattered pants. "The wanderlust has faded. I regret nothing. I seen the entire country and lived like a free man. But the truth is, I'm not sure I can make it another winter out in the cold."

"Say the word, and I'll take you to the local YMCA now and help you find a job."

"But you need me here."

"I can use Buddy or one of the other guys, Gunner. Just tell me which one you think's the most trustworthy."

Gunner shook his head. "Nah, sir. I'm going to earn my keep and fulfill my end of the bargain."

"Promise me you'll be careful. Trust no one," Liam warned. "Not even the cops."

Especially the cops. For the crimes to go on for so long, they were either turning a blind eye or, worse, they were ringleaders.

"If there's any danger, call me and I'll swoop in. Still got your phone?"

Gunner fished it out of his jacket pocket and held it up proudly. Thank heavens for the government policy that made it possible for the homeless to be given free cell phones. It was a lifeline for them, a connection to the world.

"Can't tell ya how grateful we are for these," Gunner said, returning the phone to his pocket.

"No problem." Not long after arriving in Baysville, he'd made sure each of the men obtained one, using the address of the nearest shelter as their place of residence.

Gunner held out a hand. "I get you info you can use on your case, and you can set me up at the Y. Deal?"

"Deal." No matter what happened, he'd find a way to convince Gunner to leave camp. He could only hope that some kind stranger had done the same for his uncle.

He reached his destination, and Gunner got out of the car. After a quick goodbye, Liam slowly eased out of the field and back onto the main road. Harper's home was just ahead and to the right. She'd probably fuss at him working in the field when he was supposed to be laid up in bed taking it easy, but Liam couldn't resist stopping in to see her.

A KNOCK SOUNDED at the front door, and midstir on the soup, her hands stilled. A quick glance at Mrs. Henley and Harper breathed a sigh of relief. Her neighbor had heard it, too. This was no phantom noise.

"You stay put. I'll get the door," Mrs. Henley said, pushing herself up from the table. "Were you expecting someone?"

Harper spotted Liam's red pickup truck in the driveway. She'd been so wrapped up talking with her neighbor she hadn't heard his arrival.

"It's Liam."

Mrs. Henley's brows rose. "Who?"

"Officer Andrews. You met him the night that truck almost ran me over."

"Ah." She grinned. "I thought I noticed a spark between y'all. Maybe he can talk you into staying in Baysville where you belong. I'll let myself out so you two can be alone."

"You don't have to do that," she protested.

Mrs. Henley winked. "Sure I do."

"If you won't stay for supper, at least take some soup home with you. I'll fix it up while you get the door."

Her heart tripped at the sound of Liam's deep voice as he crossed the threshold. And when he entered the kitchen, the sight of his tall body and gray eyes that smoldered like gunmetal set off butterflies in her tummy. Harper tried to rein in her smile. Liam had no business driving all around town with his injury.

"You shouldn't have—"

"I'm fine."

She wasn't so sure. "You have no business driving with that injury."

"What injury?" Mrs. Henley cut in.

"Have a seat," she ordered Liam, pulling out a chair.

"It was nothing. A minor—" he began.

"He was shot in the leg yesterday."

Mrs. Henley gasped. "What's the world coming to? People actually shooting at our police officers." She shook her head as she accepted the plastic container of soup from Harper. "Thanks, dear. And you be careful, young man."

"Yes, ma'am."

"Smells amazing in here," he said after she'd left. "What have you been cooking?"

"Sautéed shrimp and she-crab soup. Hope you don't have a shellfish allergy."

"You could have picked up fast food burgers for tonight and I'd be happy—as long as we're together."

The warm glow flowing through her body had nothing to do with the kitchen heat. Damn, even his voice sent her heart rate into overdrive. "I better stir the sauce."

She returned to the stove, checking the burner. It was a bit of an obsession with her to closely watch the stove. One kitchen fire was enough for a lifetime.

"To answer your earlier question, I was speaking with Gunner and the other homeless men at their camp down by the railroad track."

"Did you talk to him as part of your undercover work, or were you taking them more food?"

"Both."

Satisfaction flooded Harper at his admission. Liam must trust her at least a little bit to divulge his business. She continued stirring, waiting to see if he offered more of an explanation.

"I'm beginning to think there's a connection between the vagrant murders and the illegal gambling and prostitution rings."

"Why?" she asked, removing the pan from the burner. Everything was ready.

"It makes sense that whoever runs them would hire transients for muscle work."

"Like roughing up people who don't pay their gambling debts?"

"Right. And making sure the prostitutes fork over a large percentage of the money they take in."

She returned to the table, shaking her head. "Hard to believe this kind of thing has been going on under our noses."

"Enough of work. What have you been up to all day?"

Liam had opened up about his undercover work; couldn't she trust him with the latest bit of weirdness at the house? Would he think she was crazy? Honestly, though, she'd love an objective opinion. If Liam believed her nuts, then there was no relationship to be built. Best to find out now.

"Actually, something did happen today," she admitted, smoothing the denim on her thighs. "It's hard to talk about. I don't want you to think I'm nuts. It only happens when I'm alone and—"

"Just tell me." He tipped her chin with a crook of his index finger, forcing her to meet his eyes. "I've heard lots of strange tales as a cop. I won't judge you. Are you hearing strange sounds again? Receive any more threatening emails?"

"More noises," she said past the burn in her throat.

No shock or flicker of skepticism crossed his face.

"If you think my train has boarded for crazy town, just tell me," she prodded.

He stood and scanned the room, as though searching out things unseen. "When was the last time you heard them?"

"Last night, before I went to the hospital to see you. I'd had a glass of wine and drifted off to sleep only to wake up to all the weird sounds. I heard more this morning, too."

Liam circled the room, eyeing everything top to bottom.

"One of the strange noises I'm hearing sounds like a pebble hitting a window. It made me flash back to the past."

"How's that?" he asked, continuing his search.

"I know I told you that I'd caught Presley sneaking out a few times at night. Once, I heard pebbles bouncing off her bedroom window. I guess a signal someone was outside waiting on her. I was only nine at the time and didn't want to rat on my big sister. Maybe if I had…" Harper swallowed hard. "Maybe Mom would have read her the riot act and Presley would still be alive."

Liam was back at her side, kneeling at her feet. "No," he said firmly. "Stop it right there. You aren't responsible. It was a horrible accident."

"Or was it?" she whispered hoarsely. "There was that *thing* standing by her body."

Liam stood. "One mystery at a time. Were you in the bedroom when you heard the noises?"

"Yes. The first time."

"And the second time?"

"I was in here, in the kitchen. Only this time it wasn't at night. No way it was a dream or the effect of a glass of wine. There's no rational explanation for it at all."

"Creepy. You must have been scared. Which no doubt was the intent behind it."

"The noises are awful—the basement doorknob rattling, hard breathing, scratching and even the sound of a child crying." An involuntary shiver racked her body. "If Mrs. Henley hadn't come inside with me, I might have driven straight to your place."

"Let's go take a look."

"At what?" she asked in confusion.

"Your bedroom, for starters. I'm going to sort this out immediately."

He headed up the stairs, and she reluctantly trailed behind him. "I don't know what you're expecting to find. I can assure you that as long as someone else is in the house, you won't hear anything unusual."

"All the more reason to be suspicious."

He breathed hard, rubbing the wound on his leg, but she knew better than to mention it. Liam was undeterred once his mind was set.

Harper gripped the polished mahogany rails as she climbed. Each step felt like hiking a mountain. Once inside the bedroom, Liam methodically scanned every corner and searched behind every piece of furniture. He seemed so out of place in the feminine room, and she was eminently conscious of her bed—the place where she'd indulged in more than one fantasy of the two of them together.

She cleared her throat. "What exactly are you searching for?"

"I'll let you know when I—" He pulled something from the top of an old watercolor painting on the wall opposite of her bed. "And here we go."

"What is it?"

"A camera," he said grimly. "Bet there's hidden microphones or speakers, too."

What did it mean? Where had they come from? Harper shook her head. "It's not mine. I don't understand."

"It's planted. Someone is trying to scare you." He skimmed his hand along the top of her dresser. "Aha! Found them."

She hurried to his side, where he extended a hand. Tiny black speakers and wiring rested in his upturned palm. Harper backed away as though he held a nest of baby vipers.

"This explains the noises."

"But—how?"

"Everything must be operated remotely by computer." His gray eyes were as cold and stormy as the autumn sky. "Who's been in your bedroom?"

"I—I don't know. Nobody!"

Liam stormed out the door and down the stairs.

"Where are you going?"

"To find the rest of them."

She scrambled after him, only to trip halfway down the stairs. One moment she was stepping on solid ground, and the next her feet flailed into emptiness. Before she could scream, strong arms grasped her beneath her legs and back.

"I've got you," Liam said.

She buried her head against his broad chest; the crisp linen of his dress shirt smelled detergent-clean, and Harper relaxed against him until the wild beating of her heart mellowed.

Liam picked up several tiny metal objects from the steps. "What's this?"

It couldn't be—yet, she couldn't deny the solid proof in front of her. "Jacks."

"Like—in the kid's game?"

She retrieved the jack from his hand and closed her fist around the six-pointed metallic piece with enough pressure that the sharp nubs indented her flesh. This child's game piece was real—nothing ghostly about its solid substance.

"Yes," she whispered. "Presley and I used to play jacks together all the time."

"That doesn't explain how they got here."

The world went fuzzy as she bent down to pick up the toys. Surreptitiously, she swiped at the wet pools that formed in her eyes. Jacks was the one game she could beat her older sister at. They'd have mammoth games of onesies, twosies and on up to fivesies, which was the edge of Presley's maximum pickup skill. As for herself, she'd practiced until she'd mastered ascending to the tenth level. She pictured the two of them, cross-legged on the bedroom floor, shrieking with glee as they picked up the pieces before the tossed rubber ball bounced down.

Harper picked up the scattered pieces, counting eight in all. "Two are still missing. The game comes in sets of ten," she informed Liam. Her eyes swept the stairs, but she couldn't locate any more.

"That's hardly the point," Liam said. "How did they get here to begin with? Did you drop them earlier?"

"I haven't even thought of jacks in years." These had materialized from thin air.

Liam shook his head. "Gaslighting. Someone is seriously messing with your head."

"But why? What would be the point? I don't have any enemies."

Harper followed him into the kitchen, where Liam began the same methodical search he'd conducted upstairs. From behind the toaster oven, he pulled out yet another camera and speaker. "And here we go," he announced in grim satisfaction.

Harper plopped down at the kitchen table, squeezing the eight jacks. The pain kept her grounded to the surreal discoveries in her home. The place where she ate, slept and bathed—all the time under the assumption she was safely sheltered from the world. Bathing… "Check the bathrooms," she croaked. Had someone seen her naked—at her most vulnerable? And if so…were they recording the images to blackmail her?

"What if there's a place on the dark web with nude photos of me?"

Liam's face darkened. "Normally, I'd say that's highly unlikely. That's not the reason why your tormentor snuck hidden cameras through your place."

She wasn't sure if Liam's reasoning was reassuring or not. No matter what, her privacy had been invaded, and she'd never feel the same here again.

"I'll check it out." His footsteps echoed through the house as she laid her head on the table and shut her eyes. If only burying her head in the sand was a real possibility.

Liam's steps grew louder, and she lifted her head.

"Good news. Nothing in either of the bathrooms."

"Suppose I should be grateful for that."

"I want the names of everyone who's been in here the past couple days." Liam pulled out his cell phone and swiped the screen.

"It can't be anyone I've let in," she protested.

His lips pursed into a straight line. "Don't count it out. Consider everyone a suspect."

"Okay. Let's see. Kimber's been over. And her crew cleaned out the basement while I wasn't home." She latched onto that idea. "Must have been someone on that crew, right? Some sicko playing a joke on me—the old crazy girl living alone in the house where her teenaged sister died. He and his friends are probably having a good laugh right about now." Anger replaced apprehension. "We'll get all their names from Kimber. Think you can pick out the culprit in the interviews? Could be the whole crew is in on the joke."

"Anything's possible," he conceded, his fingers flying over the keypad as he made notes. "Who else has been here that you know of?"

"Nobody."

"That's not true. Mrs. Henley just left."

"Lurlene Henley?" She gave a disbelieving laugh. "You can't be serious."

"Oh, but I am. Deadly serious."

"She's a sweet old lady who's lived across the

street from me all my life. A friend of my mom's. What possible reason could she have for gaslighting me?"

"If she has a motive, we can find out. Anyone else?"

"A delivery man was here yesterday afternoon, but he was never out of my sight when he set a heavy package in the foyer for me."

"That's it?"

"Yes."

Liam clicked away and then returned the cell phone to his back pocket. "I'll report this to Bryce and have a couple men do a thorough sweep to make sure no more cameras or speakers remain."

"Thank you."

He regarded her silently.

"What?" she demanded.

"Didn't you tell me your friend wanted to buy this house?"

"Yeah. So what?"

"How bad does she want the place? Enough to scare you into selling?"

"That's ridiculous," she snapped. "We've been best friends for years. Kimber's a highly successful Realtor. Buying my house will hardly make or break her business."

Liam dug out his phone once more. "What's her last name again?"

"Collins," she said tightly. "As in Collins Realty."

"Got it."

"It's not her. Don't blame Kimber."

"We'll see."

"I don't want you antagonizing my friend."

"If she's got nothing to hide, then she won't mind a few questions to help us get to the truth. As your friend, she'll have your interests at heart."

Harper sighed. Damn his logic. "You make an excellent point. Can't argue that."

Liam nodded with satisfaction. "Great. Because I don't want to argue with you. What do you say we enjoy our dinner and table this discussion for afterward? Frankly, I'm starving."

"Doubt I'll enjoy a bite. Must be nice to compartmentalize your emotions," she grumbled. Although, to be fair, the ability to do so must make his job a heck of a lot easier.

Liam's hand rested on top of hers. "Whatever we discover, remember that the truth is never as painful as living a life in fear."

She nodded. "You're right. It's hard to even sleep here at night anymore."

"Stay with me, then." His gray eyes smoldered as his thumb stroked her hand.

"But I can't—"

"Just stay with me—at least until all this is over."

"No. It doesn't feel right. Running away never solves a problem."

"You'd be doing the Baysville Police Department a favor. They'll still be patrolling my house at night until we discover who shot at us. If they also have to do drive-by patrols of your house, it will be stretching them thin."

She hesitated.

"Do it for me?" He shot her the sexy smile she found hard to resist. "I have enough to juggle without lying awake at night worrying if you're safe. Plus, together, we'll be stronger."

"In that case, I accept."

Chapter Eleven

K-i-m-b-e-r C-o-l-l-i-n-s.

Liam hit enter on the keyboard and waited while the Baysville PD's computer network packaged bits of data in cyberspace, searching for a recognizable hit. Not that he expected anything. Harper was confident that her friend was aboveboard and a well-respected member of the community who'd been born and raised here.

He had enough years of law enforcement experience to recognize that a prestigious pedigree had no bearing on a person's morality. Ethically challenged or desperate people came from all walks of life.

While he waited, Liam read the updated file on his desk regarding the Allen Spencer investigation. Two more underage girls had come forward as victims. The judge had set a very high bond for Spencer, but despite any support from the community, Spencer had rounded up the money and was now out awaiting trial. He was forbidden any contact with minors and had been dismissed from his church.

Ding. The tiny beep signaled the computer had

found some sort of match. Liam clicked on the rap sheet PDF document and quickly scanned its contents. Four counts of check fraud, all within the last month. So, Harper's friend wasn't the entrepreneurial success she imagined. Or maybe Kimber just lived way above her means and it had finally caught up with her. It wasn't like Kimber Collins had committed a violent crime, but she was no angel, either. These weren't merely bounced checks—she'd written them fully aware there were insufficient funds in her bank account to cover the amounts. The bounced checks totaled over five thousand dollars, and she'd written more than three in a five-day period—which made the charge a felony instead of a misdemeanor, punishable by a two-year sentence. Currently, she was on bail for the offense.

He tapped a pencil on his desk, pondering the implications. From his office window, he watched as a couple of trustee inmates raked leaves. A loud rap on his open office door shifted his attention to Bryce, who leaned against the door frame, a scowl etching his face.

"You shouldn't be here," Bryce ground out. "You're no good to any officer if we're called out for a disturbance. Matter of fact, you'd be a hindrance."

"That's why I'm sticking to paperwork. Limited-duty stuff for a couple more days." He met Bryce's scowl. "You're welcome," he added sarcastically.

Bryce pushed away from the door and sat in a chair opposite him. "What kind of paperwork are you doing?"

"Filing incident reports, taking complaint calls. That kind of thing. Figured I'd help out doing what I could."

His boss had the grace to look contrite as he opened a stick of clove-flavored gum. "Appreciate that," he mumbled, stuffing the gum in his mouth.

"Any specific reason you wanted to see me?"

"Heard you'd arrived for work, so I wanted to warn you not to go out on calls."

"Hadn't planned on it."

"Good. Because as it stands now, you're a liability."

At least I'm an honest cop—unlike you. But Liam bit back the words. "I'll consider myself warned to stay put."

"Good." Bryce nodded, apparently mollified that his authority had been validated. "Dad and I are going out for a bite to eat. Want me to bring you back a burger? It's the least I can do for an injured officer."

The conciliatory offer caught Liam by surprise. "No, thanks, I'm meeting Harper in a bit."

His boss didn't make the usual eye roll at the mention of her name. "Surprised she hasn't left town yet."

"Why should she be in any hurry?" Liam stared his boss down. "Seems to me that someone wants her to leave pretty badly."

"What are you talking about? That phantom email warning her to get out of her house?"

How much could he probe his boss for information? "That and a couple other incidents, like the truck nearly running her down," he said, keeping any other information vague. "How well do you know Kimber Collins?"

"I've known her all my life. She's married to Richard, a good friend of mine. Why do you ask?"

He gave a nonchalant shrug. "I was reviewing the arrest log, and her name jumped out at me since she's friends with Harper."

"Right. They appear to be in some financial straits lately."

"What kind of work does her husband do?"

"Sells insurance. I thought he'd been doing well with it. Guess the bad economy's getting to all of us."

"Maybe. Or maybe Richard, or the both of them, have expensive vices."

"They live in a beautiful house and drive nice cars. Their kids go to the best private school in the area—so I bet the bills all add up while their income's taken a hit. No need to suspect anything more dire than that."

"Or it could be your friend has a problem." Liam decided to test the waters. "Like drugs or gambling or even taking up with hookers."

Bryce flushed crimson and jumped to his feet. "Richard wouldn't cheat on his wife. He's crazy about her. He might drink a bit—but drugs? No way."

He noticed his boss skipped one of the vices he'd mentioned.

"What about gambling, then?" Liam pressed. "I've heard rumors there's some big-time action taking place right under our noses."

"First I've heard of it."

Bryce was lying. His face had gone from crimson to pale. Either he was incredibly naive, stupid—or part of the problem. Liam's money—if he were a betting man—was that his boss was well aware of everything that happened in Baysville. But he said nothing while Bryce gained his composure.

"I'll put my ear to the ground. Even ask Dad if he's heard the same rumors. If you get any concrete leads, fill me in."

Like hell he would. "Of course, boss."

With a satisfied nod, Bryce sauntered away.

About time he headed out as well. A quick burger and then he and Harper had a date to meet Kimber Collins at her office, ostensibly to get the names of her crew. But he wanted more than that, although he'd have to exercise caution. Harper was already angry he thought of her friend as a suspect, and now he'd learned that Richard was buddies with Bryce.

Small towns often made for sticky social situations.

THE INTERIOR OF Collins Realty vibrated with an understated elegance. From the expensive crystal chandelier to the plush carpeting and mahogany furniture, it telegraphed glamour and wealth. Not the unattainable kind of wealth—but a step above the run-of-the-mill kind of American dream. Harper cast an appreciative glance at the cream-colored walls and the splashes of turquoise and coral accent pieces that offset the heavy masculinity of the dark furniture.

A place both men and women would be comfortable as they discussed the finer points of house bids and mortgage rates.

"I wasn't expecting you to bring company," Kimber said, her eyes flitting from Harper to Liam.

Harper gave her a reassuring smile. "This is my friend Liam. We had lunch, and I invited him to come along and meet you. Hope that's okay?"

"Of course." Kimber nodded and gestured at the white sofa. "Have a seat and I'll get you the crew list on my desk. I've printed it out."

This already felt awkward, and Liam hadn't even said a word yet. Must be the police uniform making Kimber uncomfortable. Harper should have asked that he wear street clothes instead. This might have been easier if she hadn't called ahead of time and told Kimber about the gaslighting attempt.

"Here you go." Kimber held out the list to her as she sat in the wingback chair across from them. "But I'm confident none of my employees had anything to do with whoever's trying to scare you."

Harper looked it over.

"Do you know the people on the list?" Liam asked.

"A couple are familiar, but not all. But if Kimber vouches for them, that's good enough for me."

"I'll run them through the police department's computer, see if any of them have a record."

"They don't," Kimber asserted. "I do thorough background searches on everyone I hire."

Liam folded the paper and tucked it in his jacket pocket. "Not all criminals have records."

"What possible reason would one of them have to harass Harper?"

"That's what we need to discover. Seems like someone's afraid of her asking so many questions about Presley and the past."

Kimber crossed her legs and casually began swinging the top one as she leaned back into the chair. Harper was glad to see her visibly relax. Of course, Kimber was assured there was nothing to fear. She'd done nothing wrong.

"'Fraid I can't help you there, Officer. But if you're ever in the market for a new home, give me a call."

"She's the best Realtor in town. She's even offered to buy my house and turn it into a B&B if I decide to sell later."

"A B&B?" Liam turned to Kimber. "Have to admit that offer surprises me. How would you have time to run your own business and think about taking on another full-time job at the same time?"

"I'd hire a manager for the B&B, naturally."

"Still would be a formidable task managing both enterprises at once. Especially initially, what with finding staff, marketing and everything else that goes into such a venture."

Kimber lifted her chin. "I can assure you, I'm extremely capable and up to the challenge."

"I'm guessing you hope the B&B would help with your current cash-flow problem."

Cash-flow problem? What was he talking about?

Harper glanced from one to the other, trying to figure out what caused the sudden tension in the room. Kimber gripped the sides of the chair, and her lips pressed into a thin white line while Liam sat unnaturally still—a lion ready to pounce on unsuspecting prey.

"What's all this about?" she asked, breaking the awkward silence. She tried to get Liam to face her, but he was intent on staring down Kimber. Resentment slashed against her ribs. He'd promised not to antagonize her friend, but he was doing just that.

Kimber wiped her hands on her navy pencil skirt and then smiled bitterly at Liam. "I see you've been checking up on me."

"It's all part of my job to be thorough. And I'm especially serious when it comes to Harper's safety. She's reported several recent incidents of hearing noises in the house."

"I would never hurt Harper." Kimber flashed her a panicked help-me-out-here look.

Harper stood. "Enough. We've got the list. Let's go."

"Maybe I've looked at this from the wrong angle," Liam said slowly, leaning back and throwing an arm across the back of the couch. His intent to pursue this matter couldn't be clearer. "Maybe everything going on at the house was an attempt to motivate Harper to sell to you."

"You've got a lot of nerve." Kimber's composure crumbled, and she leaped to her feet, shaking in outrage. "I've known Harper all her life. Who are you

to come in here and fling such wild accusations?"
She switched her gaze to Harper. "You believe me,
don't you?"

Harper opened her mouth to say yes, but the word
stuck in her throat. She glanced at Liam, and something in his sturdy, calm demeanor gave her pause.
Gray eyes pleaded with her to have a little faith in
him. How could she deny Liam the benefit of the
doubt? After all, he'd trusted in her from the very
beginning, even when his boss insinuated she was
mentally unstable. She drew a deep breath. "I think
we should listen to what Liam has to say."

Liam's eyes glowed with silent appreciation, but
Kimber gasped as if she'd been slapped across the
face. She pointed at the door. "You can both get out
of my office. I won't be insulted and accused of
something I didn't do."

"We found hidden cameras and speakers, Kimber. If I ran tests, would your fingerprints be on that
equipment?"

"How dare you! I should sue you for harassment!"
Despite her forced anger, her red lips trembled, and
she abruptly sat back down.

Harper noticed that Kimber hadn't answered Liam's question outright, though, and her heart sank
at the betrayal by her friend.

Liam leaned forward, as though moving in for the
kill. "If I got a search warrant to have all your home
and office computers and cell phones and other tech-
nical devices examined for evidence—"

"You have no grounds to invade my privacy on such flimsy evidence," she scoffed.

"If you have nothing to hide, then why not let our computer and audio forensics guy take a look?"

"I have a lot of confidential information on my computers, about clients. I could never let you go through them without a warrant." Kimber turned her gaze from Liam and faced Harper, and her normally cool blue eyes were as frightened as a cornered kitten. "You believe me, don't you, Harper?"

She cast a glance at Liam. "You believe she's guilty?"

"Yes."

Who to trust? She didn't want to believe Kimber would play such a nasty trick on her, but desperate people did desperate things. "I don't want to believe it's true," she admitted at last. "But if it *was* you, please tell me. I need to know the truth."

"Come clean and this will go easier on you," Liam urged.

"I wouldn't press charges. Just be honest."

Kimber regarded them silently and then keened forward, dropping her head onto her knees. Beneath the cotton fabric of her shirt, her shoulders shook. Harper stood stiffly, watching the woman she thought she knew get herself together.

Kimber lifted her head. "I'm so sorry." Her voice was strangled, and her cheeks were smudged with black mascara. Nothing like the poised, in-control Kimber she was used to seeing. But then, perhaps she'd never seen the real woman until now. Before, she'd always regarded Kimber as her savior wrapped with a mantle of kindness.

"Why?" she whispered past the lump in her throat.

"We need the money. So bad. Richard gambles. It started small—a few bets on sports games between friends—but then it escalated over the years. It got so bad I took him off our credit cards and hid the checkbook from him. Somehow, he always finds a way to get the money, though."

Harper picked up the box of tissues on Kimber's desk and pressed one of them into Kimber's hand.

"We're about to lose everything, even our house," Kimber confessed. She blew her nose and swiped her face, which only served to make the black smudges worse. "I—I thought I could make a success of the B&B. Even with all of us living there, we'd have a couple of spare rooms to rent out. Plus, I was hoping to eventually add on more rooms through reconstruction."

The Collinses' beautifully restored farmhouse. A showcase home that she'd painstakingly decorated for a decade. And now Kimber was about to lose it all. Pity tamped down her initial anger at Kimber's deceit.

"Why didn't you tell me all this earlier? I would have listened. I wouldn't have held out for a better deal."

Kimber shrugged her shoulders. "I was trying to fix our problems without Richard's business being affected. And...pride? I know how you always looked up to me. I didn't want you—or anyone—to know just how bad it's gotten."

"Bound to come out when your check-fraud cases go to trial," Liam said drily.

"I keep hoping for a miracle," she admitted. "I know. It's stupid. But I can't bear everyone knowing I've failed."

"You'd rather torment me out of my own home than have everyone know you aren't perfect. That's pretty sick."

"I don't blame you for being angry. I would be, too."

She had to get out of here. Harper grabbed her purse and strode to the door.

"You aren't pressing charges—right?" Kimber's voice rose. "Isn't that right, Harper?"

She should reassure Kimber, but her heart wasn't in it. Not yet, anyway. Let her sweat it out a bit. After all, how many nights had she lost sleep—too afraid to sleep in her own bedroom? All because of Kimber.

On the porch she closed her eyes and inhaled the crisp clean air.

"You okay?" Liam draped an arm across her shoulders.

The heavy warmth spread comfort through her body—a balm for her troubled spirit. "I should go back in and reassure Kimber I'm not pressing charges. Right?"

"It's okay to think about yourself now. She betrayed your trust. I wouldn't be in any hurry to offer comfort if I were in your shoes."

Chapter Twelve

Home.

It felt great to be back, to know that she was safe inside her childhood home. The danger had been eliminated. Police officers had come by earlier today and done a clean sweep of the house. No other cameras and speakers were found. So no more hunkering down at Liam's place.

How could Kimber have done such a thing?

Resolutely, she tamped down the anger and upset. Kimber had caused enough trouble—she didn't need to waste any more of her time dwelling on that confrontation. She ran her hands along the smooth oak table that had been there ever since she'd been a little girl. Happier times when the whole family had been together. Her gaze drifted to the fireplace mantel in the den and the large photograph of the entire family smiling the kind of bright, carefree grins one sported before life kicked you in the butt.

And then she noticed something else. *That* smell had returned. Only a trace, but enough that her nostrils flared in distaste. She'd deal with that again another day. For now, she'd fix iced tea and then head to the master bathroom for a long, scented bubble bath. Only two years earlier, Mom had installed a whirlpool tub to help ease the pain of her arthritis, and it made for a lovely retreat.

She poured a glass of tea and reached into the cookie jar to grab a snack, but only crumbs remained. Her brow furrowed. She'd just filled the jar a couple of days ago. The officers who'd searched her home must have helped themselves. Which was fine—the least she could do to show her appreciation. Tomorrow she'd send a written thank-you letter to the police department. In the bathroom, her mom's old radio, now dusty, sat on a shelf, and her eyes were magnetically drawn to the old-school device. How many times had she and Presley heard Mom playing classical music from this very room? Some people retreated from life's demands by taking a nap or settling in front of the TV with a cup of coffee, but their mom had opted for long bubble baths and classical music. Really loud music. Mom had been deaf in one ear, the result of a childhood infection.

On impulse, she retrieved the radio and pressed play. The invigorating chords of Johann Strauss's "Blue Danube Waltz" blared in the small space. A memory, long forgotten, surged forth—she and Presley impromptu waltzing through the house to this very piece. What they lacked in elegance they made up for with youthful enthusiasm as, hands on each other's shoulders, they leaped and skipped about the kitchen and hallways.

Nostalgia, bittersweet as baking chocolate, smacked Harper's senses as she filled the tub with hot water. What was that old saying—in for a penny, in for a pound? Might as well go all the way for the full effect. She located Mom's old bottle of gardenia-scented bath salts before stripping down and stepping into the tub.

Heavenly. The stress of the day began to ease as she enjoyed the water's warm, liquid caress. Mom's method of escape was a winner. She closed her eyes, imagining herself dancing at a Viennese ball, the Danube River flowing magically in the background.

Everything would get better now. No more strange voices and unsettling emails. No more treacherous friends manipulating her mind. To top it off, Liam was quickly healing from his wound, and their relationship grew deeper every day. Languidly, Harper traced her lips with an index finger, recalling his kisses. In many ways she was a lucky, lucky girl.

A loud rustling erupted from outside the bathroom window. Shrubbery scraped against the frosted glass pane. A small animal, perhaps? But no, a cat or dog couldn't cause that much ruckus.

But a human could.

Fear prickled along her neck and shoulders, and—despite the bathwater's heat—her arms broke out in goose bumps.

A silhouette appeared—a broad outline of head and shoulders. She wasn't alone. Frantic, she glanced at her robe hanging on a hook on the wall and out of arm's reach. Much as she loathed stepping naked out of the tub, lying there like a sitting duck for the

Peeping Tom was an even worse option. With a giant splash, she climbed out, snatching the robe from the hook and wrapping the tie around her waist.

"Get out of here! I'm calling the police right now."

Rounded eyes and a gaping mouth regarded her from the other side of the glass. Even through the distortion of the frosted window, something in the shape and angle of his face seemed familiar. Anger melted her fear. Did everyone in this town have a hidden sinister nature underneath their masks of smiles?

The man vanished.

This probably wasn't the smartest thing to do, but if she wanted to know the creep's identity, this was her only chance. The guy was fleeing after all, not trying to break in and harm her. Harper flung open the window.

She recognized that slight-built frame. "Hey!" she shouted. "What are you doing here, Allen?"

His head whipped around, his eyes wide pools of panic. He froze, head twisting from side to side, as though debating whether to flee or face the music.

"Get back here," she ordered. "Talk to me before the police arrive. Might go better for you this way."

Allen's shoulders slumped, and he shuffled back to the window. "Damn it."

"Is that anyway for a preacher to talk? Oh, that's right," she continued, voice dripping in sarcasm. "When he's caught peeping in a woman's window, that's the least of his worries."

"It's not what you think," he protested, holding up

his hands like a shield. "Please don't call the cops. Please. I'm already in enough trouble."

"Why should I care?"

"If not for me, then will you do it for my family? My wife and kids will be devastated. Give me a chance to explain."

This ought to be good. Harper crossed her arms. "You've got one minute to explain yourself."

He glanced around the yard. "Meet me on your porch? In case anyone walks by and wonders what I'm doing. This doesn't look right."

She laughed. He'd been creeping around in the shrubs by her window and *now* he was worried what people would think?

"Don't you dare run off," she warned.

"I won't. I can explain this misunderstanding. Meet you around front. And make sure you put some clothes on first. I have a reputation to maintain."

The nerve of that sanctimonious hypocrite.

Quickly, she threw on a pair of jeans and a T-shirt and ran to the front porch. To her surprise, Allen hadn't left. He sat in the glider, awaiting her appearance. Anyone passing by would think he'd come to pay a call, exercising his pastoral duties.

The creep.

"I thought teenage girls were more your forte. Why were you peeking in my bathroom window? Only one answer comes to mind."

Allen winced. "It's not what you think. I didn't know that was a window on a bathroom. Really. Sit down and let's talk."

"I'll stand right here, thank you very much."

"All right then." He drew a deep breath and exhaled loudly, running a hand through his thinning hair. "I was just trying to find you to talk. Your car's in the driveway, so I knew you had to be home. I knocked at the front and back doors for over a minute, and you didn't answer."

"Which would lead anyone normal to figure that the person was indisposed for company."

"I wanted to take advantage of this moment. You're either not home lately, or that *cop*"—he practically spat the word—"is with you."

"Anything you have to say to me, you can say in front of Officer Andrews."

"Not really. You see, he's the problem."

She quirked a brow, waiting on his explanation.

"He's ruined my life. I was fired from my church, and my marriage is in shambles. I'm facing financial ruin, too. No one would help me in posting bond. You have no idea what it's been like for me."

"Spare me your sob story. Wouldn't hurt my feelings if you hadn't been released on bond. I'm worried about Emily and any other victims that might turn up during the investigation."

"I'm begging you, Harper. Talk to him and see if he can help me out in some way."

Allen was delusional if he thought there was anything Liam could or would do to help him.

What had Presley ever seen in this creepy wimp? "Preying on minors is breaking the law. You should be put in jail."

"I never admitted crossing a certain line. What I did was wrong, but I can seek treatment. Start over."

"She's a child. Don't try to justify anything to me. And I'm really supposed to believe you weren't trying to enjoy the show in my bathroom?"

"I couldn't see anything through the frosted glass. You're not going to tell him about that, are you? I was only trying to find you."

A shudder of revulsion passed through her. "Stay away from me, Allen. Don't ever come back here."

"For Presley's sake—can't you at least grant me a little kindness?"

"You're pathetic. Even you admitted she'd broken up with you weeks before she died. You have no claim on my pity."

"What if I told you I might have information?"

A pulse of nervous energy sparked in her chest. "Like what?"

"You came to me wanting to know if I got her pregnant. I didn't. But I know who Presley was secretly seeing after she broke up with me."

"Who?"

Allen wagged a finger. "First, you agree not to tell Liam I was at your bathroom window. Second, I want special consideration when my case comes to trial."

"I'm not agreeing to anything. Give me the information or give it to Liam. You know you can't keep it secret."

He gave a long-suffering sigh. "All right, all right. What do I have to lose? I've lost almost everything anyway. But if you could see it in your heart to help me, put a word in for me…"

"Who was it?" she demanded.

"Bryce Fairfax."

THE PHONE RANG, and he recognized the caller number. Liam pressed the Answer button on his vehicle's Bluetooth device. "What's up, Gunner?"

"I've been contacted."

Finally. A break in this case. "By who? What did they ask you to do?"

"He didn't give me his name. Guy come down to camp, and I seen him chatting up with Buddy. But Buddy shrugged him off and walked away. He don't cotton to strangers, you see. Then the guy goes over to Buddy and I stroll over real quiet like to see what he's up to."

Liam grit his teeth in exasperation. All he needed was the man's description and what he wanted with Gunner. But he'd learned not to interrupt Gunner once he'd started a story; it would only take him twice as long to gather his thoughts and start the whole story all over again.

"When he mentioned a job enforcing dudes to pay their gambling debts, why, I motioned Buddy to walk away, too. Then I eased up next to the fella and told him I'd be interested in making a little cash."

At Gunner's brief pause for breath, Liam jumped in. "Did he give you an assignment already?"

"I'm getting to that, boss. So, when I told him…"

Liam pulled over to the side of the road and

grabbed pen and paper to write down information. Absently, he rubbed a hand over his gun wound that was more uncomfortable than truly painful. He'd find the bastard responsible for this.

"Then *he* says that I didn't look fit for the kind of job he had in mind. He needed muscle to man-handle a welsher. Ticked me off big-time. I told him I was scrappy and had won many a fight at camps over the years. That I could hold my own with any-body. Guy didn't look convinced but said he'd give me a test job. Pay me one hundred dollars, cash, to go rough up this dude who needed to be taught a les-son. And I says…"

Liam couldn't stay silent. "What's the target's name?"

"The target? Oh, you mean who I'm supposed to rough up? Well, I'm getting to that. So, I told him I wouldn't take any less than one hundred and fifty bucks. You know, just to make it seem like I weren't too interested in taking the job. Didn't want him to be suspicious of me. So the guy agreed to that. Gave me fifty bucks and said I'd get the rest tomorrow when I completed the job."

Liam's heart hammered with anticipation. "Who are you supposed to beat up?"

"Well, at first he didn't want to give me a name. Just an address. But I told him I needed at least the target's name, and a photograph would be even bet-ter. Told him I wanted to make sure I didn't hurt the wrong man, see? I could tell he didn't like that, but he got out his phone and showed me the guy's picture.

Looked like a real preppy kind of dude. Know what I mean? Fancy clothes and a trendy kinda hairdo you don't get at a real barbershop. Must have gone to a girly beauty parlor to get it done, know what I mean?"

"Go on." Liam refrained from banging his head against the dashboard. But just barely.

"Did I tell you the guy also said there might be an occasional need to force a call girl to pay up all the money she'd collected? Now, I draw the line there. Told him so, too, but that I'd find someone willing to do it. And he said, what are you? King of the hobos? And I said…"

He glanced at the dashboard clock. He was already late meeting Harper for dinner, but work came first. If they continued seeing each other, she'd come to realize that grim reality. Could be a deal breaker for her, but it wouldn't be the first time a woman had decided that he wasn't worth the aggravation. Although he quietly admitted to himself that if Harper felt that way, it would shake him.

"Anyway, we exchanged cell phone numbers. I'm supposed to call him after I finish the job."

"Excellent. Give me his number. Probably a throwaway phone, but I'll check it out." He scribbled down the number Gunner provided.

"How's this going to work now, boss? What's gonna happen when I don't show up for the job? Makes me a little antsy to have this guy ticked off. Worried he might come hunt me down."

"I'll contact the target and squeeze him for information on the players in this racket. Hopefully, we'll get this shut down quick. In the meantime, I'll pick you up now and take you to a safe location."

"I appreciate that, boss, but wait until tomorrow. If I suddenly leave it'll look funny to my guys. And what if this man shows up at camp again in the meantime and I'm not here? It'll blow up everything."

Gunner was right, but Liam didn't want to place him in a vulnerable position. "I'll take that chance."

Gunner chuckled. "Truth be told, I kinda want to spend tonight with my friends. One last time, ya know?"

"Are you sure?" This didn't sit well with him. The old man played a dangerous game.

"Positive." In a sudden show of brevity, Gunner added, "Gotta go. Meet me about four o'clock tomorrow at the clearing. Oh, and the target's name? Richard Collins."

Collins…a jolt of recognition coursed through him. Had to be Kimber's husband. Time to pay the man a visit earlier than he'd planned.

He was so close. Liam could almost feel the answer to his questions settle into the palm of his hand. Squeezing the steering wheel, he eased his truck back onto the road.

Chapter Thirteen

"Where are you headed?" Liam's voice called to her from the cab of his vehicle as Harper descended her porch steps to her car. She was on her way back to Kimber's to reassure the woman she wouldn't press charges. As angry as Harper was, she knew Kimber was hurting, and she didn't want to inflict pain on her when she herself had suffered enough.

After sharing this news with Liam, his eyebrows shot up. "Not a good time," he said stonily.

"Why? Are you headed there? I could go with you."

"It's police business, Harper. I just happened to be heading past your place."

She sighed. "Tell me. You know I'll find out soon enough. And you won't stop me from heading there, too."

When he explained his mission, she got in his car without asking permission. "I can help," she announced. "Richard and Kimber know me, and they're in my debt for not pressing charges. Besides, I need to get out of the house."

"Why? Did anything happen?"

On a sigh, she told him. "Allen Spencer paid me a visit earlier."

Liam scowled as he drove. "What did he want?"

"The usual. For us to back off."

"No way."

"That's what I told him."

Liam grasped her hand and raised it to his lips, kissing the inside of her wrist. "This meeting with the Collinses won't take long," he promised. "And if anything else is bothering you, we'll work it out."

She gazed out the passenger window until she spotted the 1830s farmhouse with its redbrick, federal-style architecture rising with a quaint charm in the wide meadow where several horses grazed. "Isn't it beautiful?" she said wistfully. "And wait until you see the inside. Interior brick walls in the kitchen, fireplaces in every room, vintage appliances—"

"Sounds like they sank a fortune in this place," he commented wryly. "No wonder they're up to their eyeballs in debt."

"Richard's gambling is at the root of their problem, not the restoration." Her knee-jerk defense of Kimber surprised her—considering how Kimber had tried to scare her out of her own home.

"They can pay off house loans, but gambling ones just get bigger and come with strings attached," she added.

"Whatever the reason, they're in serious trouble," he said.

Liam pulled into the semicircular cobbled driveway and stopped the car. "Why don't you wait here while I conduct my police business? What if Richard doesn't react well?"

"All the more reason to go in with you. He'll react better if I'm there as a reminder of what he and Kimber owe me for not pressing charges," she countered, exiting the car. They walked up the pathway to the front door.

"You should see this place in spring. Kimber planted roses and herbs along the border, and it looks and smells like heaven."

But Liam didn't respond. His jaw was set in determination—a look she'd come to think of as *full cop mode*. He pressed the doorbell, and they silently listened to the deep chime echo inside. Moments later, a pigtailed girl in Hello Kitty pajamas opened the door and stared up at them with welcoming curiosity alight in her eyes—the same shade of blue as her mother's.

"Miss Harper!" she threw herself on Harper, wrapping her small arms around her thigh.

"Hey there, Courtney." Harper smiled at the child's enthusiastic welcome. "Good to see you, hon."

"Who's at the door? I told you not to answer it unless…" Kimber emerged from the den and then stopped in the hallway, surprise and uncertainty clouding her eyes.

Liam had felt that an unscheduled visit would be more strategic. That way, he could speak without an attorney or anyone else from the Baysville PD involved.

"May I have a word with you and your husband?" Liam asked.

Kimber's hand flew to her throat. "Go back in the den, Courtney."

They all watched as the little girl raced down the hall. Once she was safely out of sight, Kimber faced them. Her eyes darted back and forth between Liam and Harper. "You aren't…" She wet her lips. "You aren't here to arrest me on more charges, are you?"

"No, ma'am. But I have serious business to discuss with you and your husband. Is he home?"

"Yes." Reluctantly, she gestured them inside. "Let's go to the sunroom, where the kids won't be able to hear us."

"Richard?" she called out. "We have company."

Harper strolled down the familiar hallway, feeling oddly…disloyal. Which was crazy. Kimber was the one who had betrayed their friendship, not her. And yet, how many times had she been in this same house, feeling like part of the family?

Not anymore.

They followed Kimber into a sunroom furnished with white wicker furniture. Baskets of lush ferns hung from the high beams. Glass panels afforded a view of the surrounding woods. At a rustic pine table, Kimber stiffly gestured for them to have a seat. A moment later, Richard appeared in the doorway, dressed casually and sporting his usual easygoing grin.

That smile faltered at their somber expressions. "What's up?"

"Shut the door. I don't want the kids to hear."

"Sounds dire." He tried to joke, but it fell flat in the strained silence. Richard took a seat, folding his hands on the table.

Liam extended a hand. "Liam Andrews."

The men shook hands, and Richard gazed at all of them expectantly.

"I did something really stupid you don't know about." Kimber's lips twisted, and she dropped her gaze to the floor.

"That's not why we're here," Liam cut in.

Richard kept his eyes focused on his wife. "What did you do?"

"I was desperate to get my hands on Harper's house. You know I've always thought it could be converted to a profitable B&B. And we need the money so bad."

Richard scowled, clearly unhappy with their financial situation being discussed openly.

"You can explain that to your husband later. Like I said, that's not why I'm here, and Harper's already told you she's not pressing charges." He faced Richard. "Actually, you're the reason we're here today. You're in deep trouble."

"Me? You've got to be joking." He snorted with disbelief. "And I don't even know who the hell you are. What's your business with us?"

Kimber tapped his folded palms in a quick warning. "He's a cop, Richard."

Chagrin washed his face. "Guess I better listen up, then."

"It's come to my attention that you've been gambling heavily—to the point where you're overdue on your losses."

"Not again!" Kimber pushed away from the table, eyes blazing. "You promised me you'd stop."

Richard looked down at his hands, and a flush crept from his neck to his face. Harper's heart went out to him. She'd never seen him look anything but carefree and confident. And she knew he was crazy about Kimber. Gambling must be a sickness with Richard, a compulsion that drove him despite his best intentions.

"Have you even been attending the counseling classes?" Kimber continued. "Or have you been lying about that, too?"

"I have. It's just… I thought a couple of wins and I could ease the strain. Pay a few overdue bills."

"Same old story." Kimber shook with indignation. "It does me no good to work so hard when all you do is gamble everything away."

Richard raised his head and faced Liam, ignoring his red-faced, accusing wife. "How did you find out about my uncovered losses?"

"I have my sources," he answered evasively. "It's reached the point where they're through with the verbal threats. Tonight, they plan to physically coerce the money from you."

Stunned silence greeted that news.

Kimber recovered first. "What do you mean?" she whispered.

"Oh, my God. What have I done?" Richard groaned and scrubbed at his face. "I'll go to the bank now and pay them off."

"What good will going to the bank do? There's nothing there. You've ruined us!"

"*I've* ruined us? What about you? You just had to buy this place and go crazy fixing it up."

The sunroom door squeaked open, and Courtney stuck her head out. "What's wrong?" she asked, her little face puckered in dismay. "Why are you screaming?"

"See what you've done?" Kimber said in a whispered hiss at Richard. She pasted on a fake smile. "Everything's all right, sweetie. Go back in the den and watch TV with your sisters."

Courtney teetered on her feet, her gaze flickering back and forth between her parents.

"Go on," Richard said gruffly. "We'll be there in a few minutes."

Their daughter didn't appear convinced that all was well, but she obediently left, her shoulders drooping as she shut the door behind her.

"Thanks for the warning," Richard said, using the table to push himself up. To Harper, it appeared his spirit had been sucked away. "I'll take precautions."

"But what about us?" Kimber faced Liam. "Are those men coming after me and the children, too? Are we in danger?"

"I won't let them touch you or the kids," Richard vowed. "I promise."

"Yeah, right. Like you promised you'd quit gambling?"

"Y'all can stay with me a couple of nights. Or until the danger's passed." Harper surprised even herself with the offer. Despite what Kimber had done, the thought of Courtney and her sisters being in danger pulled at her conscience. She had plenty of room at home, and it was only for a short time.

"You'd do that for me after…after everything I've done?" Kimber swiped at the tears streaming down her face.

"I want Courtney, Anise and Layla to be safe," she hedged. Harper turned to the scowling Liam. "Won't this make it easier for you to set up a sting tonight?"

"Maybe," he conceded.

"I can handle this on my own. I don't need your help. Or any…sting operation."

They all stared at Richard in disbelief. Liam was the first to recover. "Suppose you do manage to dodge an enforcer tonight. What about tomorrow night and then the next night? You can't be with your wife and children 24-7."

"Don't be stupid, Richard. Accept his help. Hear him out." Kimber lifted her chin in determination. "If you don't, I'm leaving you. I won't subject my children to danger. We'll go, and no judge will ever award you custody. Care to gamble on that?"

Richard sat down abruptly, shoulders rounded in defeat. "You don't understand."

"Enlighten me," Liam urged.

"You can't beat city hall."

"Meaning?"

"Why do you think this gambling operation has

lasted so long?" Richard said with a sigh. "I can give you the name of the guy that manages the poker games and who collects our cash. But it won't do you much good to lean on him. He's bragged before that his job is risk-free… The cops are in on it."

LIAM HAD SUSPECTED as much all along, but his first reaction was a knee-jerk denial that the men in blue were so corrupt.

"And I don't just mean they turn a blind eye," Richard continued. "They're over the whole thing. You see my predicament. There's no escape for me but to pay them off."

"How do you know that for sure?"

"Rumor," he admitted. "But it makes sense, doesn't it?"

It did. Liam drummed his fingers on the table, debating his options and quickly discounting telling Richard that he worked undercover. Should he call in the big guns now? His gut screamed no. Until he apprehended the enforcer paying Gunner, he had no proof of anything. He needed to bring in the enforcer and wrangle a confession in exchange for fingering the masterminds. Folding now would severely jeopardize his chances of bringing down the criminals.

"Can't you put a hidden mike on Richard at a gambling game?" Kimber suggested. "Get the guilty to incriminate themselves?"

"Are you trying to get me killed?" Richard asked with a snort. "Divorce isn't enough for you?"

"There's a better way," Liam suggested. "The best

chance of arresting the head of it all is to put the screws on the middleman. Which in this case means catching the enforcer in the act of getting paid off."

"You mean be willing to let some dude beat the crap out of me and then arrest him for assault? No, thanks."

"Hear me out a minute—"

"No way." Richard stood again, grimly shaking his head. "Y'all can leave my house now. I've heard enough."

"Cooperate with Liam," Harper urged quietly. "We don't have the money to buy your way out of this mess. And even if we did, what about the next time you lose? Liam's offering you a way out."

Richard sank back in his seat, and Liam shot Harper a grateful look. She knew this couple well, and they trusted her to have their best interest at heart.

"Do it, Richard." Kimber briefly laid a hand on her husband's shoulder and then faced Liam. "You promise to keep him safe. Right?"

"I will."

Harper rose. "Why don't we pack overnight bags for the girls and head over to my place?"

Liam gave her a grateful nod. She'd instinctively realized he'd have a better chance of talking Richard out of acting alone if he was out of earshot of his wife.

"Thank you. That sounds like a good idea." Kimber nodded, seemingly eager to get away.

"Call me in a bit," Harper said to him. "We'll go over the plan."

He nodded.

Kimber cleared her throat. "Goodbye, Richard. Stay safe."

"Do you really care?" he asked gruffly.

They stood and faced each other; their hands, like magnets, seemingly drew out to one another and their fingers entwined. Despite the hurt and pain, it was obvious the couple was still in love. The two men watched as Kimber and Harper left the sunroom.

"What's the game plan?" Richard asked, running a hand through his short shock of hair. "I'll do anything to keep my family from being hurt by my stupidity."

Could he trust this man not to call Bryce the moment he left? Harper had warned him that Bryce and Richard were friends, that they'd played on the same high school football team for years. But those high school days were long gone, and he'd witnessed the way Richard looked at Kimber and his daughters. The man cared about them.

"If you don't one hundred percent cooperate with me and keep your mouth closed, I'll arrest Kimber for criminal mischief."

"Kimber? What the hell did she do?"

"Long story short, she planted cameras and speakers at Harper's house, trying to scare her into leaving Baysville and selling her the property. Your wife is obsessed with the idea of turning the place into a

B&B. She seems to think it's the answer to your financial problems. Sell this place, move into Harper's house and then rent out the extra bedrooms."

"She'd be willing to sell our farmhouse?" Wonder flickered in his eyes. "She loves this place. More than she loves me, I suspect."

"Doesn't sound that way to me. She was desperate to fix this problem."

For the first time in their visit, Richard's eyes lit with hope. "Whatever you have in mind, I'm game."

"First thing I need is for you to tell me who collects the gambling money," he said.

"Fair enough." Richard gave a long sigh. "The man's name is Mitchell Sullivan. He's the pharmacist that owns the Baysville drugstore."

Liam's brows rose at the name, although nothing should surprise him in this line of work. Greedy people came in every socioeconomic level. "And Sullivan takes these payments at his place of business?"

"Yep." Richard ran a hand through his hair. "We text him when we arrive, and he goes around to the back door to collect our money that's discreetly folded inside plain-covered envelopes. He treats it as though it were a business transaction. Which, I suppose one could argue, it is."

Chapter Fourteen

Liam kept his sight on Harper as she led Gunner through the dark woods. He didn't like her being here, but she'd insisted, and he was afraid if he left her out, she'd turn up on her own, increasing the danger to herself.

Water squished around his feet, threatening to suction him down into the swampy morass. His socks slightly dampened inside the supposedly waterproof boots. Good thing he'd brought along a spare set for Gunner, although the guy was probably used to wet socks and much worse. Luckily, the moon was close to full, providing plenty of light as they made their way along the back edge of the properties. The flip side? The full moon made detection easier.

He stayed well behind them, trying to keep his footsteps quiet and his back bent in a crouch when they hit clearings between the woods. Gunner claimed not to need a backup as he hiked to the Collinses' farmhouse, that it was bad enough he had to follow Harper, but Liam insisted on providing protection. He had an uneasy feeling about this.

Something swooped nearby, and a small limb broke off a tree less than ten feet away. Must have been an owl. Liam drew to a complete standstill, ears straining, but there was only the rustling of trees and shrubs and an occasional, far-off dog barking. Even Harper and Gunner barely made any noise as they quickly walked along. Harper was familiar with this area and had mapped out the direction earlier for them but insisted that they still needed her eyes as they hiked unfamiliar territory.

At long last, a light shone from the clearing ahead. This was it. Liam observed the tall, thin lines of Gunner and Harper as they quickly strode to the designated area of the Collinses' farmhouse and lifted a window that had been left unlocked and slightly ajar.

There was no reason for the tingling at the back of his neck. Nor any explanation for the foreboding that filled his gut with dread. Yet, Liam couldn't shake the feeling of being watched.

A scream erupted from the farmhouse. "No, don't! I'll pay. Stop!"

Even though the entire scenario had been prearranged down to the smallest detail, including the fake begging for mercy, his unease continued to mount. Could be that the enforcer had a policy of watching the first assignment of a new recruit and they were all being observed from somewhere in the darkness.

Shadows shifted and moved. To his right, a tall, muscular person, dressed entirely in black, slipped from behind the trunk of a large oak and sprinted across the field. As the man was a good fifty yards away, Liam couldn't make out any identifying details. The figure again disappeared into the night. Seconds later, the sound of a motor roared to life. An elliptical beam of headlights strobed the field and woods—and then the vehicle sped down the county road.

Once the engine noise faded away, Liam walked directly to the farmhouse and knocked on the back door. No need to hide any longer. As he suspected, the enforcer spied on his newest henchman. What was he to make of Gunner having a companion? Hopefully, the guy wasn't *too* concerned as long as he'd witnessed Gunner fulfilling his end of the bargain. The enforcer probably assumed Gunner had brought along one of his homeless friends.

"Who's there?" Gunner called out behind the door.

"Liam. All's clear."

The door immediately swung open, and he entered. Both men stood in the kitchen, anxiety palpable in their agitated stances. Harper leaned against the counter, looking calm and confident. As though she had done this a dozen times before. The woman had unplumbed depths.

Richard hurried to lock the door. "Anyone see you out there?"

"Probably not." Liam wished he could offer more assurance. "But, Gunner and Harper, y'all were being watched. Not long after you entered, a man slipped out of the woods and took off in his vehicle. Once I was sure he was gone, I came."

"We heard the engine, too." Gunner shook his head. "These guys mean business, don't they?"

"Once you get the payment, I'll arrest the enforcer," he promised. "Agents will wire money into your bank account first thing in the morning to cover the debt. After the arrest, I can call in for backup."

"The state guys, right?" Richard asked. "The local police will do more harm than good."

"They're standing by for my call. After tomorrow, we'll have at least two arrests. The enforcer paying off Gunner and the man accepting your gambling payment. Between the two of them, I'm confident at least one will give a full confession."

Richard nodded, but it was clear he didn't share Liam's full confidence. But if he were in Richard's shoes, he'd also be uneasy until the matter was resolved.

Harper took off the knitted black cap she wore, and her red hair gleamed in the light. "I'm glad this is almost over. I still can't believe Mitchell Sullivan is involved in all this. I didn't see that one coming."

Gunner leaned back against the sofa and ran his weathered hands along the smooth leather. "Nice home you got here. Must make you right proud."

Richard shrugged. "It's been a hell of a strain. Feels good to finally admit that truth. I'm tired of keeping up pretenses. Time for me to get serious about straightening up my problem and getting my family back to normal."

"That will be a relief to Kimber," Harper muttered.

"I ain't never had much, but I've seen more of

this country than most men," Gunner said quietly. "It's been a grand ride, but I'm ready to settle." He grinned. "About time for someone my age, eh?"

The two men clinked their beers.

"Sorry to interrupt the bro-fest, but let's get to work." From his inside coat pocket, Liam withdrew a large, white cotton strip of cloth and a small box of makeup. "Lucky for us, it's Halloween season. Every store is carrying rows of monster makeup. Figured we can use this to draw a black eye. The cloth is for a makeshift sling. Might consider slightly limping on one leg when you meet Sullivan, although we don't want to overdo it with the acting."

Richard dubiously eyed the makeup kit. "I'll wear dark sunglasses so he can't see my eyes too closely. Maybe just a purple smudge peeking through the bottom rim."

"Perfect. I've got a small mike for you to wear under your shirt. Damn shame we can't do video, but it's too risky."

"Sullivan doesn't usually say much. Matter of fact, he doesn't even open the envelope in front of me."

"Then you say something short, like *here's my payment from last weekend's game.* See if you can draw him into a conversation. Maybe take off your sunglasses for a second and remark that you've learned never to be late again."

"Gotcha."

"Text me as soon as you get back in your car." Liam turned to Gunner. "And you text me as soon as the enforcer answers your message about meeting him for the money. Arrange for the payment to take place at camp, if you can. Hiding out in one of the tents will be easier for me than if he tries to draw you out to some remote area in the woods."

"Got it, boss."

"I've already reserved a bed for you at the YMCA and lined up a job interview at city hall. They need a good maintenance worker."

Gunner cleared his throat. "I won't let you down, boss."

"I know. Again, I'm offering you my spare bedroom tonight. Just to be safe."

"Take it, Gunner," Harper urged.

"Nah, I'll be fine with the other fellas. We look out for each other. Ain't nobody sneaking up on me."

"If you're sure." Liam didn't like it, but he couldn't force the man into accepting his protection, either.

"I wouldn't mind y'all driving me back to camp, though," Gunner admitted. "These old legs of mine are mighty tired from all that walking tonight."

Richard offered Gunner his hand. "Thanks for helping out. And thanks, Harper, for all you've done, too. I'm fortunate y'all took the job. Otherwise, I'd have gotten my ass kicked tonight in front of my wife and kids."

"We all got what we wanted, including Liam." Gunner tipped up the beer can and finished it off. "Guess I should be heading on back."

Richard hustled to the kitchen. "Let me pack a to-go box for you." From the fridge, he pulled out sandwich meat and cheese, adding it to a bag where he tossed in chips, bread and canned goods. "Take the beer with you, too," he urged.

"Don't mind if I do," Gunner said with a grin. "We'll all have a grand time tonight at camp."

HARPER OPENED THE door of her house, and she and Liam were greeted with the children's shrieks.

Kimber rushed to the foyer. "How did everything go? Is Richard okay?"

"He's fine. Everything pretty much went according to plan," she assured her.

"*Pretty much?* What's that mean?"

"Like I said, Richard's fine." No point mentioning the enforcer had seen her enter the farmhouse. It would only needlessly worry her friend. Besides, there was nothing to be done about it now. Liam gave her a quick nod; they were in accord on this.

"Guess I'll be on my way," he said, edging toward the door.

Harper regarded him with suspicion. What was his hurry?

Kimber unexpectedly threw her arms around Liam's neck. "Thanks for everything," she said gruffly. "If anyone can help Richard and me, it's you."

"No problem."

"Back in a minute," Harper told Kimber, following Liam out the door. "You don't have to run off. Why don't you stay for supper?" she asked.

"Got a couple things I need to check up on."

She pursed her lips. "You're going to keep an eye

on Gunner tonight, aren't you? I'll go with you. We can take turns sleeping on your stakeout."

"You should stay with Kimber. She needs a friend tonight."

"She's a grown woman. I'm coming with you."

Liam cocked his head at the front window where Kimber's face was pressed against the glass, blue eyes huge with worry. The girls had joined her, their faces taut. "Grown or not, deserving or not, she needs you. So do her kids."

Harper sighed and threw up her hands. "If you're sure. I'll be glad when this is all over tomorrow. Whoever's behind this crime ring has to be the one responsible for shooting and chasing us."

"Exactly." Evidently mindful of their audience, Liam only gave her a reassuring hug before heading to his vehicle.

Back inside, Kimber had flopped into a chair and dropped her head in her hands. If Harper was tired, then Kimber was a total wreck. Judging from her swollen, red eyes, Kimber had been crying for hours.

"Girls, why don't you go upstairs a few minutes while I talk to your mom?"

Kimber straightened and pasted on a weary smile for them. "Go on and take a bath and get in your pajamas. I'll help you in a few minutes."

The girls left, albeit reluctantly.

"Richard hasn't contacted me," Kimber said, her voice rough. "We could go back tonight, but if he wanted us, he'd have called by now."

"He's probably scared to—or ashamed. Y'all

didn't part on the best of terms. And he does want you to be absolutely safe here."

"But he should call me. I'm not the one who got us into this mess."

"This mess isn't one hundred percent his fault, is it?" she asked gently. "Surely, you two can work it out."

"I'll admit I've spent way too much money over the years, but the majority of this *is* Richard's fault. I thought when he finally agreed to counseling that we'd turned the corner, only to discover that he's lied to me yet again."

"It's your marriage. You know best." Who was she to offer advice or to judge?

Kimber nodded and blinked back tears. "I don't deserve your kindness. I'm truly sorry. It was horrible of me to try and scare you off with those noises."

"For the last time, apology accepted."

"Can you really forgive me?"

"Yes." And it was true. The trust had been broken and she'd probably never feel quite the same about her old friend, but Harper was willing to let bygones be bygones.

The doorbell rang, and Kimber's hand flew to her chest in alarm. It was as though she expected any second for someone to burst through the door and harm either her or her kids.

"Relax, I'll get the door. It's probably the pizza I ordered." Harper opened the door and stared in surprise. "Richard?"

A chair scraped in the kitchen, and a set of squeals

erupted in the den. "Daddy! Daddy!" the girls cried as they ran to the door. They threw themselves against him as Kimber watched with widened eyes.

Richard stepped through the door and faced Kimber. "Are you ready to come home?"

Kimber looked ready to put up a fight, but instead, she ran to her husband and hugged him, the girls at their side.

Harper felt her own eyes moisten. This family was going to be okay, she just knew it. Silently, she retreated from the foyer to give them privacy.

Minutes later, a sheepish but much happier Kimber and Richard entered the kitchen, arms around each other's waists.

"I'm taking my girls home," Richard said, a grateful gleam in his eyes. "Thank you for letting them stay with you. We owe you."

"Glad to do it. You're welcome to stay for dinner. I ordered two large pizzas."

Richard pulled out a twenty-dollar bill and pressed it into her palm. "Thanks, but we want to get home. You understand."

Eagerly, the girls bounded to their rooms to pack their things. In record time, the family left, and she was alone once more. But at least now she could join Liam at his stakeout.

She headed up the stairs to change into dry jeans and socks, but stopped midway, blinking in surprise at the metallic glint on one of the steps. Slowly, she bent down and picked it up.

Another jack.

She turned it over in her hand, tamping down a frisson of fear. *Must have missed it earlier,* she reasoned. Yet both she and Liam had examined the staircase more than once to see if they could find the two missing jacks. *Stop. Just stop.* They'd simply overlooked the tiny object.

Harper pocketed the jack, quickly changed clothes in her room and headed back into the night to find Liam.

At the railroad camp, his car headlights were on bright, illuminating the dark in all directions. What kind of quiet stakeout was this? Something was very wrong here.

Harper parked next to him, jumped out of her car and ran. "What's happened? Are you—"

Liam approached, his arms raised. "Don't come any closer. You don't want to see."

His warning came too late. She peered around him and spotted Gunner, facedown on the ground, blood seeping through his shirt.

Chapter Fifteen

Once again, Harper found herself back in the chilly, sterile atmosphere of the Tidewater Community Hospital. Inside the generic visitor waiting room with its plastic cushioned chairs, stale coffee and dog-eared magazines, she and Liam were the lone occupants. Did anyone even remember they were here awaiting news from the surgeon?

She pushed open the door and stared up and down the empty hallways. After the frenzy of the emergency room, the surgical waiting area had the silence of a morgue. Where was that doctor? What was taking so long?

Liam pushed past her and paced the halls, glaring every ten seconds at the closed doors leading to the operating room. She leaned in the doorway watching him as images of Gunner's battered, bloody body replayed in her mind like a series of snapshots—Gunner sprawled facedown in the dirt, his cotton T-shirt shredded with slash marks, his fingers clawing into the ground, the smashed cell phone by his side. Liam had bagged a few gum wrappers for the forensics team, which arrived at the camp in short order.

Worse was what *wasn't* at the scene—not a single man remained. Apparently, they'd each packed up their meager belongings and hopped a train car out of town. All that remained of the camp was a pile of burned wood and empty food containers.

How could they leave their friend like this? Unless they'd been terrified and believed Gunner already dead. It had been a near thing. It was a wonder, given his age, that he'd survived such a brutal attack.

If Liam hadn't checked on Gunner, the man would have had no chance of recovery. But Harper could tell from Liam's haunted eyes that he blamed himself. She went to him and slid an arm around his waist. "Gunner's getting the best care possible," she said softly. "He's a tough ole guy. My money's on him to make it."

"This is all my fault. I never should have left him alone." Liam's voice was raspy, and he ran a hand through his cropped hair.

"Don't do this to yourself. You tried to get him to stay. He didn't want to."

"The enforcer realized Gunner was an informant playing a dangerous game. And I'm the one who put Gunner in that position."

"You were trying to get to the bottom of the corruption here in Baysville. Self-recrimination accomplishes nothing."

He let out a frustrated sigh. "You're right. This attack only makes me more determined to bring in the state police ASAP and get answers. First thing in the morning, I'm confronting Bryce."

"Bryce?" A ripple of surprise shot through Harper. She released her arm from Liam's back and stepped in front of him. "Confront Bryce about what?"

"He can't be blind to what's going on in his own town. I'm ready to lay my cards on the table and see what he's got to say about everything."

"I hope you're wrong." Bryce had a cocky attitude, but she remembered the sweet boy Presley once tutored, and now she knew her sister had had a relationship with him.

"Actually, so do I. But if he's in on it, I'll try to break him down."

"Or Mitchell Sullivan," she reminded him. "Still can't get over that one."

"We owe that bit of the puzzle to Richard Collins. And at least now we know why the homeless men were killed. Their deaths are directly tied to the gambling and prostitution rings."

Harper stared at the closed doors down the hallway. "I want the name of the man who stabbed Gunner."

"Cowardly bastard, attacking an old man from behind. It perfectly fits the pattern of the other homeless deaths with those stab wounds in the back torso."

Her skin crawled to think of it.

"Of course, this investigation will be much easier *if* Gunner lives and *if* he can describe the attacker."

The operating room doors swung open, and a man

in surgical scrubs strode forward. "You're the cops awaiting news on my patient?"

Harper didn't bother to correct his assumption they were both cops. She wanted to be with Liam when he got the news on Gunner's condition. She tried to assess the doctor's demeanor for a clue, but he merely looked professional and courteous.

"Did Gunner make it through surgery?" Liam asked.

The doctor nodded reassuringly. "With flying colors. His right lung was nicked, but we cleaned out the fluid buildup and inserted a tube to drain any residue. Also performed a blood transfusion to replace the lost blood, and then a mass of stitches to close the stab wounds. Despite his age, he's in stable condition and the prognosis of recovery is excellent, provided he doesn't develop pneumonia."

The heaviness in her chest lifted, and she let out a deep breath. "When can we see him?"

"He's being wheeled into recovery now. Normally, we don't allow visitors until later. Y'all need to ask him about the attacker?"

"Yes. Police business."

The doctor motioned for them to follow him. "This way."

They strode through two sets of double doors, down a corridor and then into a room filled with white gowns, hairnets, masks and slippers.

"He should be rousing from the anesthesia any moment. Ask your questions and then leave. My patient needs his rest."

The doctor led them to a room of curtained cubicles and pushed open one of the curtains. "In here."

Gunner looked as frail as Harper had ever seen him. His eyes were shut and his face was as pale as the white cotton bedsheets. An IV was attached to one arm, and he was hooked up to several monitors. They watched the rise and fall of his chest, loath to wake him from much-needed rest.

"Gunner?" Liam whispered. If Gunner didn't rouse easily, Liam would wait until he woke and was placed in a regular room. These killings had taken place over a decade. What difference did a couple more hours make?

Liam cleared his throat. "You doing okay, buddy?"

Gunner frowned, and his forehead creased in wrinkles. "Wh-what?"

"It's me. Liam. Harper's here, too." He stepped next to the bed and rested a hand on Gunner's thin forearm. "You gave us quite a scare. But the doctor says you're going to be fine."

Gunner gazed blankly at them and then at the IV needle in his arm. Harper laid a hand over his trembling fingers, offering quiet reassurance as Liam questioned him.

"You were hurt last night, and now you're in the hospital. Do you remember what happened?"

Awareness dawned in his wide, frightened eyes. "So much pain," he murmured hoarsely.

"I'm sorry. But I need to know. Did you see who did this to you?"

Gunner licked his lips. "Just for a sec. Don't know him."

She and Liam exchanged a quick glance over Gunner's prone body. So the attacker wasn't the enforcer who had originally contracted Gunner to go after Richard.

Gunner struggled to rise and then sank farther into the bed. "The other fellas? Are they…?"

"They're fine," Liam reassured him. "You were the only one attacked. Tell me what you remember."

"We'd all finished supper. It was dark. A text came, saying, 'Got your money. Meet me behind your tent.'" Gunner stopped and drew a couple of deep breaths.

"You're doing good. Just a few more questions. What happened when you met him?"

"Someone grabbed me from behind. And then… pain."

"Did he say anything?"

"No."

"Any idea how tall he was, or did he have a tattoo…anything?"

"Beefy guy. Not fat. And not young, either. Gray in his hair."

The description wasn't much help. It could be almost any man over the age of forty. "Okay, then. Rest up and I'll check back in with you later. When you're better, maybe you can give us more details and look through some mug shots."

She gave his hand a gentle squeeze, and they

walked away from the bed. Harper was about to close the curtain when Gunner spoke again.

"Don't you do it."

Liam's forehead creased. "Meaning?"

"This isn't your fault."

Liam inhaled sharply. "You'll never again spend another night out in the cold and in danger. I promise you that."

THE DRIVE HOME was silent and tense. He pulled into her driveway, and she turned to him, wanting to offer comfort. "The worst is over. He's going to be okay, Liam."

"Yeah. No thanks to me." He gave a mirthless laugh, the heaviness of recrimination obvious.

"Don't. You can't protect everyone all the time. It's not your fault."

"Exactly what he said. Which only makes me feel worse."

"Come on inside and let's talk."

"No. You go on to bed. I'm dead tired."

"Then come in and sleep with me." The words slipped out of her mouth before she had a chance to think through the implications. And by *sleep* she meant *make love*. But it felt *right*. She longed to run her hands through his hair and kiss away the sadness. She wanted to become one with him, to experience him in every sense.

She loved Liam.

The knowledge burst onto her consciousness, full-blown and irrefutable. She wouldn't tell him the words tonight—she wanted her declaration un-hampered with the tragedy of the stabbing. But she could show him love with her touch…with her body.

"Please say you'll come," she urged again.

His hesitation stretched on, but at last he got out, slamming the truck door shut. As they walked to the porch, she could see the exhaustion pouring from his lackluster eyes, unsmiling face and slow gait.

Harper sensed a certain guard from him, as if he were deliberately erecting a barrier. She'd never fallen for a cop before. Not even close. Liam seemed unable to divorce his feelings from his job tonight. Which was completely understandable. His compassion was one of the reasons she loved him. If she wanted to be a part of his life—and she did—then she needed to accept this was part and parcel of Liam. But how best to help him?

In the foyer, she leaned against him, resting her head on his broad chest. "Gunner's lucky to have you in his corner."

"Lucky?" He snorted and took a step back. "That's not the word I'd use."

"Want to talk about it?"

"There's nothing else to say. Probably best I go on home. I don't want you dragged further into this."

He was pushing her away. "I wish you'd stay," she said quietly.

"Why? I wouldn't be good company tonight."

"No problem. You don't have to be. I only want to be with you."

For the first time this evening, Liam's face softened, and he reached for her, pulling her back against his chest. His arms wrapped around her, and he stroked her back in long, firm caresses that left her craving more. Her skin tingled at the warm strength of his body through the thin cotton fabric of her shirt.

This.

This was where she was meant to be—in his arms. She cradled the sides of his face in her palms, feeling the abrasive scruff along his jaw. So masculine, so sexy. His mouth found hers, and the world faded to black as their lips and tongues danced. Heat bubbled in her veins, and she couldn't get close enough. She untucked his uniform shirt and ran her hands up his bare back. Muscles rippled beneath her fingertips, and his breath became jagged. Growing bolder, Harper moved her hands over his chest and then lowered them to trace his sculpted abs.

Liam stilled and pulled back a few inches, nailing her with the intensity of his smoky gray eyes. "Are you sure about this?" he asked, his voice ragged and deep.

Harper knew exactly what he was asking—and what she was offering.

In answer, she rose and held out her hand. "I've never been more sure of anything in my life."

Chapter Sixteen

Liam quietly entered Bryce's office, where his boss was engrossed in reading a file that lay on his desk. With a flick of his wrist, Liam forcefully shut the door. Bryce looked up, startled.

"What's the meaning of this, Andrews?" he asked with a scowl. "I'm busy."

"I think you'll want to hear this."

"Make it quick. I'm buried in paperwork."

"Maybe you should spend more time in the field and less time in the office if you really want to do your job effectively."

Bryce slammed the file closed. "This is *my* office, and *I'm* the chief. You'd do well to remember that. But now that you're here, answer this. What in the hell were you thinking arresting Mitchell Sullivan?"

"He collects money generated from a huge, illegal gambling ring that's been operating right under your nose for years."

"Mitchell?" Bryce scoffed. "I find it hard to believe that a man of his stature, a pharmacist, no less, would get involved in some penny-ante poker games."

"Make no mistake. This is no small-time ring. It generates thousands of dollars of income. It's even expanded into a profitable side business involving prostitution."

Bryce crossed his arms and leaned back in his chair.

"But I don't have to tell you all this, do I? You know what's going on."

"Why should I believe anything you say? You've been lying to me since the day you came in this office for a job interview. Should have trusted my instincts not to hire you."

His secret was out. Liam lifted his chin. "You call it lying, I call it doing my job."

Bryce's face flushed with anger, and he stood, glaring. "Why did you come to Baysville in the first place?"

He countered with a question of his own. "How did you find out I was working undercover?"

"Dad has lots of connections after decades working as an arson investigator. He'd worked with law enforcement agencies on a number of cases. One of his old buddies in Richmond ratted you out."

Liam made a mental note to bring Carlton Fairfax in later for questioning. "How long have you known?"

"Almost from the beginning."

No wonder his boss seemed to have taken an instant dislike to him. And no surprise Bryce was always trying to usurp his authority. His turf had been threatened.

"Why haven't you confronted me with that info before now?" Liam asked curiously.

"What's that old saying—keep your friends close but your enemies closer?"

"I'm not your enemy. We should both want the same thing. A town free of organized crime."

"Of course, that's what I want, too." Bryce sat back down. "Damn it, Andrews, why do you think I took this job?"

"Ego? You wanted to prove to your dad that you could run this place like he used to run the fire department?"

It'd been clear to him from the start that Bryce appeared to have an odd relationship with his father. The old man was always around, offering advice. It was as though he regretted ever retiring and wanted to continue running what he could behind the scenes.

A tiny muscle worked in Bryce's jaw, and the pencil in his hand snapped in two. The sound detonated like a firecracker. A stunned silence followed.

"Looks like I hit a nerve," Liam remarked drily.

"What's all this crap about organized crime? I assumed you were sent because you state guys found it suspicious we hadn't solved the homeless murder cases."

"It's what caught our eye at first," he admitted. Liam debated whether to say more, but he decided a friendly talk with Fairfax might elicit more info. The full heat of his division would be bearing down on Baysville by this evening or early morning at the latest. And he wanted to be the first to interview the chief, tap him out and observe his reaction to the pressure. "The murders are our top priority. But now I'm convinced the murders and gambling and prostitution are all related."

The angry flush on Bryce's face melted, replaced by a sheet of pasty white.

"You don't like my theory?" Liam pressed.

"I don't see any possible connection between the two crimes."

"Whoever the ringleader is, he's been hiring the homeless over the years to enforce people to pay their debts."

Light dawned in his boss's eyes. "And you think he later killed the men he'd hired to ensure their silence."

"In his eyes, they're an expendable commodity. Use them for a bit, then when they've seen too much or start asking questions, it's time to kill. After all, they're the perfect victims. Nobody reports them missing or brings public pressure to solve the case. Sometimes the victims aren't even identified."

"That's a lot of theorizing on your part. Where's the evidence?"

"Why should I show my entire hand to you?" The irony of using a poker analogy wasn't lost on Liam, but he plowed on. "Start talking. Prove to me why I should trust you."

"I'm not going to defend myself from your outrageous insinuations."

"Outrageous? Explain your reasoning."

"The murders have been spaced out over the

years. And all the victims are transients. You know as well as I do that these people have a high rate of drug and alcohol abuse and mental illness problems. Those issues lead to violence. They're constantly vulnerable to becoming crime victims."

He thought of his uncle Teddy. "Doesn't mean their lives matter any less."

"I'm not saying that."

"Really? Because it's our observation that this department hasn't been aggressive in their investigations. I came to find out why."

"Not true. I've done all I can to solve the murders."

"Have you?"

Bryce slammed a fist on his desk. "How dare you. You feds think we have unlimited personnel to chase down clues? I do the best I can with the Baysville budget."

"Not good enough."

"Are you accusing me of incompetence—or something even worse?" Bryce pulled a stick of gum out of his pocket, popped a wad in his mouth and began chewing furiously.

Liam's gaze affixed on the crimson and white stripes of the discarded wrapper, and then his eyes slowly traveled up to meet Bryce's dark eyes.

"What?" Bryce asked, bewildered.

Liam grabbed the wrapper and studied it more closely, then held it to his nose. The scent of cloves was pungent. Yes, this was it. A perfect match.

"I found wrappers just like this near Gunner's body," he said softly.

"So?"

"So I collected them as evidence, and it's been sent to the forensics lab in Richmond."

"You won't find my prints on them. Anyone could have dropped those wrappers at any time. Not like I'm the only one who buys this particular gum."

"It's a bit unusual. An old-fashioned brand. I haven't seen them in the stores much since I was a kid. And you always seem to be nearby when there's trouble."

Bryce's expression set into defensive stubbornness. "I'm not a murderer."

"But you know who he is, don't you, Bryce?"

His mouth worked the gum as he chose his words. "I've had suspicions over the years. Nothing I can prove."

"It's a cop, isn't it? Come clean. You protect a dirty cop and you'll only go down with him." His gut clenched as he recalled finding Gunner near dead, blood seeping out and darkening the back of his shirt. Liam couldn't even imagine the pain and suffering resulting from the multiple stab wounds. He'd vowed to protect Gunner and the other homeless men from sick predators. It was the least he could do after failing so abysmally last night. "I promise I'll make you pay if you could have prevented these attacks and did nothing," he threatened.

"I'm not defending a dirty cop. I interviewed Mitchell Sullivan extensively yesterday, and he denied all accusations. Apparently, he owns a home-remodeling company on the side and Richard Collins was paying him cash for an overdue bill."

"Did you ask to look at his accounting books?"

"Of course. He said he'd have his attorney provide that."

"He's lying. We'll crack him when the full force of the agency bears down on him."

"Good."

Liam eyed Bryce curiously. "I thought Richard Collins was your friend. You believe Sullivan over Collins?"

Bryce shifted his gaze to the window and steepled his fingers. Liam waited for his answer, sensing that the man was wrestling with a hard decision.

"Sometimes," he finally said, his voice heavy, "it's hard to know who to believe. Who to trust."

Liam sensed an opening. Bryce was struggling with something, and if Liam played his cards right, he'd find out what it was and how it connected to the activities he was investigating.

"We started on the wrong foot with each other, Bryce. What do you say we work together to bring down these criminals? Just tell me what's troubling you. I promise to listen and not make any judgments until all the facts are in. You'll find I'm a fair man."

Bryce nodded, but continued to face the window, as if expecting a miraculous solution to his dilemma.

"You know something, don't you?" he prodded.

"It's all suspicions. Nothing concrete."

"Listen. Wouldn't you rather talk to me than the

suits who will be descending later from Richmond? Gunner will be shown photos of every cop on this force. If he recognizes one of them as his attacker, all hell is going to break loose in your department. At a minimum, you'll be fired and lucky to find any kind of security job in the future."

"To hell with that. My problem's a lot stickier than a damn job."

"Spill it."

Bryce scrubbed his face and then nodded slowly. He swallowed and looked down, and for a moment, Liam wondered if the man was about to cry. His eyes glistened as he spoke. "If there really is a hotbed of illegal activity connected to the homeless murders, then you're looking in the wrong place."

"I know your knee-jerk reaction is to protect your fellow—"

"The culprit isn't on the force."

"Then—"

"You need to be looking at an ex-firefighter."

Ex-? His mind spun as though he were on a high-speed carnival ride. His thoughts slowed and oddly settled on the image of one man. "You're not saying—"

"My father."

Carlton Fairfax.

Was Bryce low enough to deflect suspicion on his own father just to throw the heat off himself? Even as he pondered the question, Liam instinctively felt Bryce spoke the truth.

Bryce abruptly stood and paced the small room. "I hope to God I'm wrong."

Liam switched tactics and spoke in a reasonable, sympathetic manner. "Lay out your suspicions and we'll figure it out together."

"It started when I was in high school. Senior year, to be exact. Life was good back then. Uncomplicated. I was dating Julie, now my wife, and had received a scholarship offer to play football at Alabama. The only blip on the screen was my poor grades in math. But with his usual determination, Dad arranged to solve that problem. My future was set."

Bryce ran a hand through his hair and stood by the window, evidently contemplating his next words. "Then everything changed. I met Presley."

At the mention of Harper's sister, a knot of concern balled in his gut. "Your math tutor, I remember. Go on."

"Presley was…how do I describe her? She was unlike Julie or any other girl I ever dated. Genius-level smart. Very shy, but in a charming kind of way." A sad smile ghosted across his face. "Of course, I was determined to break down that studious wall of reserve."

"And so, you did." Liam paused before continuing, as he realized the implications of what he was learning. "You're the mystery father Harper's been trying to find."

Bryce returned to his seat. "It was a shock when she came to me with the news. Damn, I was so stupid. And careless."

Liam studied him objectively, sensitive to every nuance in Bryce's body language and voice. "Did the news anger you? So angry that you murdered Presley?"

"No. Never." He vehemently shook his head. "I would never have hurt Presley. She was adamant that she wanted to have the baby. At first, I tried to talk her out of it. I told my dad what had happened, and he exploded. Said giving up my scholarship was sacrificing my future. He had this grand delusion I could make it as a pro quarterback. Truth is, I never even enjoyed football all that much. A pro career was his dream, not mine.

"Anyway, we met that night—the night she died. After I'd had a day to absorb the news, I came over to talk with her and make plans."

"Where did you meet her? What did you tell Presley that night?"

"It was bitter cold, so we met at her house." A sheepish look flashed in his eyes. "Her mom was a little hard of hearing, which helped us from being discovered. Usually, she'd sneak out and meet me around the block, where I'd be waiting in my car. But this time, as arranged, Presley left the back door unlocked for me. When I came, she was there waiting, and we quietly slipped down to the basement. We were two scared kids, sitting on the rough, unfinished stairs, whispering in the semidarkness about what we were going to do. She hadn't even told her mom yet, because she was afraid of disappointing her."

Bryce's face was haggard, steeped in that long-ago memory. "But at least, for that one night, I did the right thing. I offered to forgo college and start working and paying child support as best I could."

Not that it mattered, but Liam was curious. "And how did Presley respond?"

"She was happy. Grateful. Promised that we'd figure it all out." He let out a long sigh. "At least I have that memory."

"And when you left—she was alive?"

"Yes."

"What do you think happened?"

"Can't say I'm one hundred percent sure. Or maybe I've pushed the truth way down deep inside. I wanted to believe that it was just an accident. She fell, hit her head and lost consciousness. The food she'd been heating on the stove caught fire. People die from freak accidents every day. Even sixteen-year-old pregnant girls."

"When did you realize it was no accident?" Liam asked softly.

"The very next day, when we heard the news of her death, Dad actually smiled. *Smiled!* It chilled me, you know? I couldn't help remembering his rant when I'd confessed about the pregnancy less than twenty hours earlier. He'd claimed Presley was deliberately ruining my life. That I should talk her into getting an abortion. When I said I wouldn't do that, he'd grown livid and stalked away. I figured he'd cool down and over time he'd accept the situation."

He'd seen and heard plenty of chilling crimes, but this murder motive was pretty horrific. "You believe your own father killed Presley and his unborn grand-child? All for your football scholarship?"

"It's what that scholarship represented to him—a way to fame and fortune." A bitter laugh escaped Bryce. "Imagine his disappointment when I went to college and ended up sitting on the bench for two years. I finally quit and came home."

"Did he ever admit killing Presley?"

"Not directly. And I was too afraid to ask him straight up. Even if he'd confessed, what would I have done with that knowledge? I was young and he was a respected firefighter—captain of the depart-ment, no less. The man responsible for investigating possible arson. The one reporters interviewed and who publicly swore it was an accident. Who'd have believed me?" He paused, overcome with emotion. "And you know what? Part of me wanted to think it couldn't be true, that he couldn't have done it. He was my father. And to imagine him doing that…"

Liam could feel for the difficult position Bryce had found himself in. Tough for anyone, let alone someone so young. Carlton sounded like a bully, a man who controlled his family by intimidation. But it didn't necessarily mean he was a murderer. Per-haps he only wanted, in some twisted logic, for his son to believe he had the power to rule every aspect of his life. He had to ask.

"What do you mean by *not directly*? Did your fa-ther hint that he'd done this?"

"For years, it was this ugly, unspoken thing be-tween us. I hoped—I tried—to believe my suspicions were ungrounded. But over the years, I became slowly aware that this gambling and prostitution ring existed. Even had a couple men tell me that Dad ran it. I finally confronted him."

Bryce stopped his tale and briefly closed his eyes. Liam leaned forward, eager to hear the rest. "What did he say?"

Bryce opened his eyes—twin pools of helplessness that fixed on Liam. "He laughed. Can you believe it? I threatened him with arrest, and that's when it all crashed down around me. He said that if I did, he'd ruin me. Dad turned on me, his own son. The former police chief, his best friend, had shown him Presley's autopsy report. Dad secretly made a copy of it and threatened to release the report revealing that Presley was pregnant at the time of her death. He'd claim that I long ago confessed to murdering her in a fit of rage. That he—a loving father—had protected me from my crime. But that now he'd had a change of heart and could no longer live with his guilty conscience. He wanted to come clean and expose my murderous crime of passion."

What a piece of work. Liam let out a low whistle. And here he'd imagined father and son were unusually close, when actually the lunches together and Carlton's presence around the office were nothing more than a form of intimidation.

"What you've told me is still not a confession of murder, though. But we can arrest your father on the gambling charges and try to wrangle a murder confession—or several murder confessions, in fact.

As I said, I believe the homeless men were killed to cover up the organized crime."

Bryce covered his face with his hands and groaned. "Dad's out of control."

As sympathetic as Liam felt for his former boss, there was work to be done. And if Bryce wanted to right the many wrongs he'd allowed to occur in the town he'd sworn to protect, then it was time to act.

"You have to make a choice, Bryce. Today. Right now. We're closing in. Are you going to help us or are you going to keep being intimidated by your father?"

Bryce sat up straight and gave a curt nod. "Where do we start?"

"Before we confront your dad, let's line up all the evidence against him. First, we'll go together to interview Gunner in the hospital and take along photos of every cop on this force, along with your dad's photo. Hopefully, he can identify his attacker. Then we'll try and force Sullivan to admit guilt and name names when faced with evidence."

Officer Combs popped his head in the door. "Hey, boss. Your dad's here for lunch."

"Tell him I'm tied up today."

Combs nodded and left.

Bryce set his shoulders back. "I'm ready. Let's do this."

Chapter Seventeen

The hot spray of water, combined with the rose-scented body wash, felt rejuvenating. Or maybe it was merely the glowing aftermath of last night's lovemaking with Liam. Today, life seemed full of possibilities. Harper could resurrect her dad's dreams of turning this old place into a B&B and hire a manager to oversee the operation. She could even sell her firm in Atlanta and reopen a new interior design firm right here in Baysville. There might not be the same pool of potential clients as Atlanta, but living expenses were cheaper here than in the big city. She could get by quite nicely with a smaller number of clientele.

Doubts suddenly assailed her. How would Liam react to all this? He might not be another commitment-phobe like Doug, but he might view her plans as being too much, too soon. But the truth was, she didn't want to live in limbo indefinitely.

And what happened once Liam wrapped up his investigation in Baysville? Nothing tied him to this town. Richmond was his base of operations. Could she handle moving from town to town while he worked various investigations? Worse, could she live knowing that every day held the possibility he might get shot? What kind of life was she contemplating?

She turned off the water, wringing her hair dry. She'd handle this one day at a time. Keep exploring her options. Have a talk with Liam.

That decided, she dressed quickly and then turned on her computer and investigated everything involved in opening a new business.

Ding. A new email notification. Her eyes scanned the list and noticed a new email that had no subject line. Probably junk the spam filter missed. She clicked on it. It was again sent from loser@life, but this time it contained no message. *Who sends blank emails?* Had to be a computer glitch of some kind. Yet her stomach cartwheeled as she remembered the earlier email warning her to get out of the house. Dismissively, she turned away from the computer and resolved to push the unsettling nonmessage aside.

She arose, stretched and faced the large four-poster bed with the rumpled bedsheets. Her thighs tightened as she remembered the things she and Liam had done there last night. He'd been a passionate, attentive lover, and it had been every bit as good as she'd imagined. Better, actually.

The best ever, in fact.

With a satisfied grin, she flung back the comforter and straightened the sheets. She ran a hand down the smooth cotton. Her fingers hit a small, sharp object between the fitted and flat sheets. An earring, per-haps? Harper turned down the top sheet and stared, bewildered at the lone jack.

And that makes ten. The last missing jack.

It hadn't been there last night. Surely one of them would have noticed if it had. No one else had been in the house today. Liam had left early for work, and she'd fixed breakfast, done a little housecleaning, then hit the shower.

And yet…there it was.

A harmless trinket from a child's game.

Harper rubbed the chill bumps on her arm, try-ing to convince herself it meant nothing. She backed away from the bed. Should she call Liam? And tell him what…she'd found a jack that was out of place? Even she smelled the whiff of crazy on that one. And she'd been taunted for years by schoolchildren call-ing her nuts…not going there again.

She wasn't ever going to permanently live in this house. B&B or not. Irrational or not. One decision down, many more to go.

Harper shoved into her sneakers getting ready to head downstairs, wanting to be near an exit door… just in case. She berated her unease, even while tak-ing measures to protect herself.

Ding.

Not again. She opened the second message from loser@life.

He'll be coming for YOU next.

Her breath hitched, and her heart pummeled against her ribs. Next? The implication was clear—someone had been after Presley.

Harper turned off the computer and went downstairs. Everything in the kitchen was as she'd left it earlier. Purse on the table, car keys lying beside it. The familiarity of everything in its proper place comforted her, but not enough to want to spend the day alone in the house. She'd escape to the friendly confines of the public library for more research on opening a new business.

The phone rang, and she jumped. An unknown number. She answered it.

"Have you talked to Andrews yet?" Allen didn't even bother giving his name before launching into his rude demand.

"Good morning to you, too. And yes, I talked to him."

"Is he going to help me?"

"That's his call, not mine."

"I promise I've changed."

What a loser. "Leave me alone, Allen. I'm busy."

"No need to be rude," he complained with a whine. "I'll let you get back to work or whatever you were doing."

Harper cut him off and began to stuff the phone back in her pocket when she heard it—a sliding, grinding noise from upstairs that pierced the silent house. This couldn't be happening. Her entire house had been swept by the police to remove any bugs.

A thump landed somewhere above her head. A

high-pitched wail rang out that was drowned by the roar of blood pounding in her ears. Running footsteps followed, and her eyes involuntarily slid to the stairs.

A pair of white stick legs appeared and—God help her, she didn't want to see more—but her traitorous gaze continued its upward trajectory, feet rooted to the floor. A thin creature stood dressed in dirty rags that hung loosely on a frame that could have been a child's or a man's or…something else altogether.

And then she faced him.

It.

The thing of her nightmares.

The thing that had hovered over Presley's broken body.

It possessed large black eyes set in an emaciated face with sunken cheekbones. Dirt smudged its white cheeks, and the hair was thin, partly balding and hung in greasy shoulder-length clumps, the ends as ragged as if shorn by a pair of child's scissors.

The smell hit her senses next. Putrid. *That explains the mysterious odors*, she thought hysterically. It was coming for her. Just like it had for her sister.

"Get out! He's coming!" it yelled.

What did that mean? Was he talking about himself in third person? She didn't aim to find out. Her body caught up with her mind's urgent scream of *danger*, and Harper raced to the foyer on shaky legs.

A pounding erupted from behind the front door. A knock that reverberated in every cell of her brain.

"Don't open that door!" it—he—yelled. The thing—the man—was closer now, at least halfway down the stairs.

Like hell she wasn't opening the door. Harper snatched it open, gulping air. She blinked at the person standing before here. "Captain Fairfax?" He was retired, but everyone still addressed him by his old title.

She couldn't have asked for a more welcome sight, unless it had been Liam—rather, that's what her mind tried to insist. But her fear only grew.

Be logical. This was the man who'd patiently investigated the fire. The first on the scene that night to save her and Mom all those years ago.

Trouble was, Harper had never cared for him. Not then, not now. Especially not coming so close on the heels of the warning still ringing in her ears.

"Who else is here?" Fairfax asked in his booming voice. "Thought I heard a scream."

She glanced behind her, but the man had disappeared. It was the past happening all over again. Except this time, it was early morning instead of late night. Which somehow made it all the more terrifying.

Yet, a calm, still voice inside her warned, *don't let this man in the house.* So what if he found her mentally unstable for an irrational refusal to invite him in?

"If you'll excuse me, I was on my way out," she lied, making a move to cross the threshold.

Fairfax laid a beefy arm across the space between

them, a barricade. His gaze shifted past her shoulder, to the kitchen table where her purse and keys sat in plain view.

"Leaving without your things?" he asked drily.

"Going for a walk," she countered, trying not to show she was flustered.

"We need to talk first."

"Okay, let's sit on the porch." She glanced at the driveway and frowned. "Where's your car?"

"Down the street," he answered evasively. "I had lunch in the neighborhood and thought I'd drop in."

He said it like this was a normal occurrence, as though they were friends who frequently visited.

They were not.

"Where did you eat? The Crab Shack? I love their shrimp tacos." She had this insane idea that if she kept him talking long enough at the door, someone would eventually stroll by and she could call out to them.

"Have you ever had their shrimp steamed in Old Bay seasoning?" she babbled on. "It's the best."

"Not here to discuss food." His mouth set into a determined line, and the yellow flecks in his brown eyes glowed in a feral manner. It made her think of hungry wolves closing in on their prey.

Don't let him sniff out your fear. Harper raised her chin and aimed for an attitude of cool indignation. "Mr. Fairfax," she said in a voice as cold and crisp as celery. "I told you I'm on my way out. Now step aside."

Gauntlet thrown.

He didn't even attempt a show of civility. "No. Get inside."

Abruptly, she ducked and tried to slip under his arm. He gave a mirthless chuckle, lowering his hand and forcing her back inside the house. Frantically, she searched the deserted street. Where was Mrs. Henley when she actually wanted to see her?

"What do you think you're doing?" Harper glared, faking a bravado she did not feel and praying that none of her fear showed through the righteous anger.

"I'm not leaving here until we've had a little talk."

Futile. She wasn't going to get past his tall, stocky frame blocking the exit. Perhaps even worse than that alarming fact was the knowledge that somewhere either behind her or off to the side—the creature lay in wait. *Be smart and focus. One enemy at a time. There must be a way out.*

And just like that, the answer arrived in a flash. Harper pivoted, racing to the back door. Her shins slammed against the kitchen table as she fled, but she barely registered the pain. There was only the roaring in her ears, the sharp, labored breath sawing in and out of her chest, and the overriding, screaming dictate to run. The command flooded her body with adrenaline.

Go, go, go.

If the creature was nearby, she didn't see it. Eyes trained straight ahead, Harper concentrated on the back door near the basement. Next to the door was a large window with a view of the backyard. A black truck was parked close to the screened-in porch. Fairfax's truck? Had he been the one stalking them all along? The sight filled her with more dread. No good reason for him to hide his vehicle from public view. None at all. She tried to banish an image of Carlton Fairfax dragging her into the truck, never to be seen or heard from again.

Or was she being ridiculous? He'd always been an arrogant, powerful kind of man. Perhaps today was only more of the same. Yet she dared not turn her head to see if he was closing the distance between them.

Halfway through the kitchen. Halfway to freedom. Her eyes locked on the prize, the cool brass knob of the back door.

Fairfax's longer, stronger arms caught up to her. He firmly laid hands on her shoulders, forcing her to turn around.

"Mite jumpy, aren't you?" he asked sardonically. "Always were a flighty little girl. Seeing things no one else can see. Hearing noises no one else hears." He gave a wolfish grin. "Oh yes, your mother told me. We talked regularly. She was quite concerned about you for the longest time. Said you trembled at every little creak and groan of this old house as it settled."

Only because she'd learned to keep her mouth shut. That way her mother wouldn't worry so much as she dealt with her grief. That way Harper could try and convince herself that all was well.

She bit her lip to stop the involuntary trembling. "Why do you want to talk to me?" She kept her voice calm and reasonable in order to appease the alarming tension that swirled around them.

"You and your boyfriend have been causing me lots of grief."

"I have no idea what you're talking about," she answered truthfully.

"Going around town, poking your nose in that old case."

"Which case?" she asked, genuinely puzzled. "The homeless murders?"

He waved a hand dismissively. "Nobody cares about those bums. World's better off without 'em."

And this guy used to be captain of the fire department? He had the sensitivity of a gnat. But she was hardly in a position to deliver an ethics lecture. "Then what case are you referring to?" she asked.

"Presley's death."

Her heart skipped a beat. "Why does that bother you?"

And did she really want to know the reason? Suddenly, she wasn't so sure. Not when Fairfax was standing so close, anger roiling off his massive body in waves.

"You don't believe her death was an accident," he stated. "You never did."

They stared at one another, and she felt herself unwilling to look away, mesmerized by the sparkling yellow flecks in his eyes.

"I have no grounds to prove otherwise," she said at last, eyeing him with what she hoped was a reassuring, steady expression.

Fairfax studied her for several moments and then shook his head. "Heard that you've stuck around Baysville this time for answers. You're determined to find out the truth."

With a casual violence that caught her off guard, he clamped a heavy hand on her elbow and pulled her.

"Hey, what are you doing?" she protested, struggling to escape his grasp. "Stop it."

He didn't even bother glancing her way as he strolled a few steps to the window and pulled the curtains closed.

The sunlight blocked, she trembled in the semi-darkness. He faced her, his hot breath washing over her face. It smelled like a musky, holiday spice she couldn't quite name. Her own breath was rapid and shallow—loud in the lull that lay thickly between them. Somewhere in the darkness, the unknown shadow dweller also breathed—silent, but watching. Always watching.

"And now we talk," Fairfax insisted. His fingers dug deeper into her elbow, hard and bruising.

Cloves, she suddenly realized. That was the spice she couldn't name. As if that mattered a whit. Perspiration dampened under her arms and her mind raced in a fever of foreboding. "Why are you doing this?" she whispered.

LIAM WAS RELIEVED to note that Gunner looked much stronger today. He sat up in the hospital bed, chowing down on roast beef and mashed potatoes. At Liam and Bryce's entrance, he swiped a napkin across his mouth and then grinned.

"They sure are feeding me mighty fine food here," he said heartily. "Three hot squares a day. And anytime I want more tea or juice they bring it right to me. Can't beat that service."

"Never known anyone to rave about hospital food," Liam remarked drily.

"And this bed's so comfortable. They've already changed the sheets, and I only been here one night."

He and Bryce shared a brief, amused glance. Liam nodded in Bryce's direction. "You've met Chief Fairfax before, haven't you?"

"Yes, sir." The happiness in his eyes dimmed a bit. Liam didn't blame him. Bryce had always acted condescending to the men at camp.

"Sorry to hear of your attack," Bryce said, extending a hand. "I'm here to make a report. We'll do everything we can to find the culprit."

A bemused Gunner shook Bryce's extended hand. "Thanks for coming out, Chief."

Bryce opened a file stuffed with papers. "Officer Andrews has filled me in on everything that's happened, including the arrangement you made to be an informant. Based on that, we've compiled mug shots of men we suspect may have been your attacker. Can you look through them and see if you recognize anyone?"

"Glad to." Gunner placed the file in his lap and riffled through the papers, brow furrowed as he concentrated on each photo.

Liam practically held his breath. Were their suspicions about Carlton Fairfax unfounded? What if he'd hired someone else to kill Gunner?

Gunner frowned and shook his head until he came to near the end of the stack. He pointed a long, skinny finger on the page. "That's him."

Liam directed his gaze downward and nodded in satisfaction at Carlton Fairfax's unsmiling mug.

Bryce wasn't as satisfied. He frowned at Gunner. "You're sure? Not a sliver of doubt in your mind? It was nighttime, after all, and your visibility was limited."

"That's him," Gunner said emphatically. "No doubt at all. Neck thick as a linebacker and dark eyes with them weird light flecks in 'em."

"Very well, then." Bryce's face was as grim and resigned as Liam had ever witnessed. "I'll send Officer Denton to come take your formal statement."

"Hey, you know the guy?" Gunner asked.

Bryce collected the file and stuffed it under his arm. "Meet you in the hallway," he mumbled to Liam.

"What's wrong with him?" Gunner asked, gesturing at Bryce's retreating back.

Liam shrugged and changed the subject. "Doctors say anything about releasing you yet?"

"Later this afternoon." Gunner looked crestfallen. "Wish they'd let me stay a few more nights. I like it here."

Which showed how abysmal Gunner's homeless status had become in his old age.

"Don't worry. You can crash at my place for a week or so. Until you're healthy again."

"I don't want to put you to no trouble."

He'd put Gunner in mortal danger, almost gotten him killed, and the guy was worried about inconveniencing him by temporarily staying in a spare bedroom. "No trouble," he answered gruffly. "I've got to run. Check on you later."

In the hallway, Bryce waited, arms folded against his chest, his expression stern. "Let's do this. We have enough to make an arrest."

"You don't have to be part of it," Liam said. "I can get another officer as backup."

"No. I want to." A muscle worked on the side of his clenched jaw. "I have to do this."

Liam nodded. He could understand Bryce's need to be the one to confront his father. "Where would we find your dad this time of day? Can you call him and make a pretense for a late lunch, a rain check on bailing earlier?"

"Don't even need to do that. I can tell you exactly where he is at this very moment." Bryce pulled a cell phone from his back pocket and his fingers moved across the screen.

"You've got a GPS tracker on his phone?" Liam asked in surprise.

"No. He forgets to carry his cell phone half the time. I put a tracker on his vehicle a couple weeks ago. After the last murder." At Liam's raised brows, he explained. "I've had my suspicions about Dad for a long time. I'd hoped this might come in useful one day."

"Ever make any connections between him and the homeless murders?"

"Nothing definite."

They began walking down the hall, and Bryce tucked the phone away.

"Where we headed?"

"Seventeen thirty-eight King Street."

Liam stopped dead in his tracks. "That's Harper's address."

"Strange. What could he possibly want with her?"

"I'm about to find out. Let's move it." Liam jogged to the stairwell, his heart thrashing in his chest—wild as an animal trapped in a cage.

Chapter Eighteen

"Why am I doing this?" Carlton asked, mimicking her words. "I overheard Bryce and Liam at the station this morning. Like I said, you and your boyfriend have caused me nothing but grief."

As if she cared about his grief. Yet she had to reason with him, appeal to his logic—however faulty. "If you hurt me, Liam will see that you pay. Think this through."

He laughed. The glee in his eyes frightened her more than the anger. *He's off. Demented.* And people thought *she* was off her rocker? No, *this* was crazy. The bone-chilling grip of the real thing was undeniable. Fairfax's glittering eyes were a portal to an abyss of madness. Against dilated pupils, the yellow iris flecks whirled like pinwheels.

"What did you hear them say?" Maybe they had figured out Fairfax was a menace. Maybe Liam was on his way now. She clung to that hope.

"I'll be the one asking the questions here." He continued dragging her, and she stumbled beside him as he strode to the den.

"What have you told Andrews about your sister's death?" he demanded, pulling the curtains closed. The house darkened another fraction.

"J-just what everyone already knows."

"That ridiculous story about a monster in the house?" Fairfax marched to the front door and locked it.

The metallic click reverberated through her like a death knell.

His lips curled in rebuke. "Your story was another lie feeding the legend about Baysville's resident shadow dweller."

With her firmly in tow, he entered the kitchen, flicking the curtain closed on the lone window above the sink. Speaking of which... She peered desperately into the dark shadows. Where had *it* gone? Hysterical giggles at the back of her throat threatened to burst, like uncorked champagne bubbles rising to the surface. Was her shadow dweller a vision of death—a grim reaper who'd collected Presley's soul and had now reappeared to claim her as well?

Still—she feared the undeniably real Carlton Fairfax more. The merciless grip on her arm, the frigid eyes and the determined ritual of curtain closing to bar the outside world. It all pierced her with the promise of pain. And the possibility of death.

He reversed direction and headed to the back of the house again. Panic spiked more adrenaline through her body. "Where are you taking me?"

He ignored the question. "What else does Andrews suspect about me?" he continued in his hard, flat voice. One she was sure he'd wielded effectively against hundreds of criminals over the years. "I'm going to get the truth."

"Nothing! Liam knows nothing, same as me. It—it was all an accident."

"That's BS."

He yanked her to move faster, and her hip slammed into the edge of the tea cart. Grandmother Claudia's antique cups crashed to the ground. Porcelain shards scattered like snowflakes on the walnut flooring and crunched beneath her feet as she was relentlessly paraded through her own house. Desperately, she flailed her free arm, searching for a heavy object. Her fingers feathered against a glass candleholder, and she strained against Fairfax's pull forward. Two inches. That's all she needed. But her fingers tap-danced on empty air. The chance to grasp a weapon vanished.

Surprisingly, Fairfax moved past the back door. She'd been certain he meant to force her into his truck. Instead, he threw open the door to the basement.

The dark and relatively soundproof basement.

"No!" She dug her heels in, throwing the weight of her body toward the ground.

Pain exploded on her right cheek, stealing her breath, as he slapped her, hard. Hot needles of pain burned like a swarm of yellow jacket stings on the tender flesh. If she survived this day, Harper was sure her face would forever bear the imprint of his palm.

"You'll tell me everything Andrews knows about me," he continued. "Right now."

"And then what?" She kicked at his shins, and the man barely even flinched. "You'll kill me like you did Presley? Is that what happened?" If she was about to die, she could at least die knowing the truth about that night.

Fairfax stood at the doorway, gazing around her house with a thoughtful expression on his face. "It all started here. With your sister."

"What started?" Her throat threatened to close on choked sobs. "What did you do to her?"

"The killings," he answered, his voice as calm as though they were discussing how to solve a math problem. "Presley was the first." He chuckled as though he'd let her in on a private joke. "Turns out, I had a hankering all along for murder. A bloodlust I'd never suspected."

"What did you do to Presley?" she whispered.

He faced her with narrowed eyes. "You really don't know? You didn't see me that night?"

"No."

He gave a nonchalant shrug. "A quick kill punch to the back of her head where the skull base meets neck. Then I placed your sister in the kitchen and started a fire. Either her body would burn, or her lungs would fill with smoke. Death by fire or smoke inhalation, depending on when my fire department arrived."

Harper absorbed the full horror of his words. She imagined Presley's terror as Fairfax raised his hand, poised to deliver a fatal blow. Harper could only hope she'd been truly dead and had never regained consciousness to find smoke and flames licking the air, an inferno from which there was no escape.

And it had all happened as she and Mom had slept a floor above. Nausea rumbled in her belly.

"It was easy," he continued in the same singsong intonation. "Took her totally by surprise. No one heard a thing."

Except she had heard something—only she could never be sure exactly what it was. She'd only known that something horrible had taken place. Mom's partial hearing loss had prevented her from waking.

Harper didn't want to hear any more details. More words that would forever haunt her if she managed to survive her own encounter with evil. Yet Fairfax's confession relentlessly continued.

"Afterward, once I'd checked her pulse to make sure she hadn't survived the blow, I picked Presley up and carried her to the kitchen. Made it look like she'd slipped and fallen on the floor while heating up a bowl of soup. Easy enough to concoct a firebomb with chlorine and brake fluid in a plastic bottle, then set that in a pan on the stove. Untraceable." He laughed. "As captain, I was the arson investigator. I made damn sure there wasn't even a whisper that the fire might have been deliberately set. After all, why would anybody question my report?"

Bastard. Fury crashed over her in waves. For what he'd done to Presley, for what he'd almost done to her and her mom.

"You left Mom and me there to die," she accused.

"I had no beef against y'all and figured you'd wake up and escape before the house went up in flames. But if not, too bad. Funny." He chuckled again. "All these years, I kept waiting for you to remember something. A buried memory."

"No," she denied again. "Not you. I saw something else."

"The monster. Right. Maybe I'm the monster."

"No. He was thin, short. He looked nothing like you."

"Obviously, your mind has distorted my image. Could that be the truth?"

"No," she answered curtly. She wouldn't be drawn into his psychological games. His need to twist and manipulate her reality. She saw what she saw.

"But I was the only one there that night. Besides, Bryce, of course."

"Bryce?" Her belly took a nosedive. "Is he part of this?" If so, she feared her chance of escape had been reduced to zero.

"No. Boy's got a soft streak. Told me he wanted to forgo his football scholarship and stay here with Presley and her baby." His face darkened. "I couldn't let him do that."

Harper twisted and craned her neck, searching for a pale face in the darkness as Fairfax continued his poisonous confession. Where was the shadow dweller? *Help me*, she mouthed into the darkness.

For someone claiming he wanted her to talk, Fairfax was the one carrying the conversation. His words poured out in an angry braggadocio. "I took care of everything for Bryce. Protected him from a nobody girl who'd tie him down forever. He had a scholarship to the University of Alabama. Do you know what that means? Do you realize what kind of opportunity that was? A chance to make something of himself. I wasn't about to let your sister ruin his chances."

"You killed Presley and your own grandchild over nothing? You're the real monster here." Worse than anything her mind could have conjured.

"After that incident, I took everything to another level with my side business."

Harper reeled at his dismissive attitude. Her sister's life, her family's pain, meant nothing to him. Instead, he acted as though Presley's murder was merely a gateway for more business opportunities.

"Somebody didn't pony up on his gambling debt? Some hooker kept too much of her john's fee? I'd hire one of those bums by the railroad tracks to force them to do the right thing."

"Murder for hire?" she whispered.

"Nah, why let them have the fun part? Let them take the risk of enforcing my rules against some local who might recognize me. I prefer to run everything in total secrecy. But if my hired hands demand more money or threaten to blackmail me, why then—I kill them. You know what I discovered? Nobody cared. No victims' family members breathing down my neck to find a killer. Hell, nobody missed the nobodies. I did the world a favor. When one of them bums got too big for their britches and demanded more money, I did what I had to do. Ain't nobody going to take what's rightfully mine. And you know what? I liked it. No, I loved it. That's right. I loved meting out my own brand of justice. To feel my knife slice through their scumbag, filthy skin. I have no regrets."

"You can't get away with this forever. If I die, Liam will hunt down my murderer like a dog."

"Dead dogs don't hunt." Fairfax laughed at his own black humor. "I'll kill you, and then next time, instead of hiring someone to take a potshot at Andrews, I'll shoot him down myself."

So that's who'd shot at Liam. No doubt he'd also been the one chasing them the night Liam was released from the hospital.

"No one will believe two women died in this same house from freak accidents," she pointed out, appealing to his brain rather than his nonexistent heart.

"They won't be able to prove otherwise. Besides, if I'm going down, you're going down with me."

He ran a callused finger from her chin to her gut.

"Too bad I can't cut you open, feel your warm blood in my hands, watch it ooze out of your body. Funny thing, I have to stab those homeless men in the back, so they don't see my face. Just in case. One day I want to run my knife down a woman. Watch her eyes as the life drains from her body. Maybe today's my lucky day."

Oh God, she had to distract him from this path. His breathing had gone huskier, and excitement crackled in his eyes. Would he lose control if he dwelled on this fantasy? Her mind scrabbled for a distraction.

"Wait! You were seen coming here today."

The excitement in his eyes melted. "You're lying."

"No. I was warned you were coming."

"Yeah, by who? Your make-believe shadow dweller?"

"He's here." Harper turned her face away. This was her one chance. He was out there, she was sure of it. She was not crazy. Whoever he was, he wasn't a killer. Fairfax was the murderer, not him.

"Help me," she screamed. "Please!"

"Shut up."

Fairfax lifted her in his arms as though she were as weightless as a rag doll, as though her kicking and flailing fell harmlessly against an armor of steel.

A flash of white materialized in the dark shadows, followed by a pop of brilliance as the lights switched on. The shadow dweller appeared, a cutlery knife clutched in one dirty hand.

"Drop her, Fairfax."

"What the hell?" he asked, bewildered.

His arms loosened, and she fell to the floor, scrabbling crab-like away from Fairfax and toward the other man.

Fairfax growled and lunged at her would-be savior. A sickening thud of flesh and bones hit the floor. He was astride the smaller man in a trice.

Outside, a siren sounded. Even though faint, she took heart that help was on the way.

She had a choice. Make a run for the door—or

help the man who'd tried to save her. Damn it. That really wasn't a choice at all.

Harper ran past both the sprawling figures and returned to the dining room for that glass candlestick she'd missed earlier. The glass felt smooth and hard in her fist as she returned to the wrestling men. The smaller guy was pinned, and Carlton had seized the knife from him. He raised it, poised for a death blow.

"No!"

Fairfax paused, glancing up as if he'd just remembered her presence. It bought her a moment. With all her strength, Harper swung the candlestick, and the blow landed on his left temple. Blood erupted and arced over her and the floor. Fairfax dropped the knife, covered the wound with both his hands and then curled into a fetal position.

The shadow dweller snatched the knife and rose.

They faced one another in the darkness as outside the sirens drew nearer. He, knife at his side, and she, grasping the bloodied candlestick holder. Behind them in the shadows, Carlton groaned.

"Thank you," she whispered. "For saving me."

"You saved me," he countered.

"We saved each other."

The siren's blare had reached near-deafening level. Blue lights strobed into the den through the curtain cracks. Any moment, the cops would burst through. This was her moment.

"You're real. I did see you the night Presley died. You were there."

"I tried to help her. But it was too late. So, I ran away and hid. Like I always do."

"Where did you hide when—"

Pounding rained down on the front door. "Harper? Are you there? Open the door, honey."

Liam. The adrenaline that had fueled her energy—for what seemed to be hours but couldn't have been more then fifteen minutes—crashed and burned, leaving her exhausted. Her legs were concrete pillars, and it took a mammoth effort to walk the twelve feet to the door and unlock it. "I'm coming," she called through the barricade.

Sunlight and fresh air touched her face before Liam pulled her in for a quick, tight hug. "You okay? Where's Fairfax?"

Liam let go and entered the den. His hand reached for his sidearm. "Who are you?" he demanded of the shadow dweller.

"Ralph." The man's voice broke, and his skinny frame trembled so violently she was afraid he'd drop into a dead faint.

"It's okay," she rushed in. "He helped me. Fairfax is on the floor by the dining room window. I—I hit him." Belatedly, she stared down at the candlestick holder she still grasped.

Bryce entered, gun drawn. "I'll watch this guy," he told Liam. "Find my...find Carlton."

She set the candlestick holder on an end table and eyed Bryce as he stood there, gun aimed on Ralph.

Presley's lover. The father of the unborn baby that

never had a chance at life. "Your dad confessed," she told him. "Did you know he killed Presley?"

Bryce didn't look at her, but the gun in his hands shook. "I suspected," he admitted.

From behind them, Liam's voice rang out. "Call an ambulance while I cuff him and read him his rights."

Oh, God. How badly had she hurt him?

"Bitch tried to kill me," she overheard Fairfax grumble.

"Too bad she didn't." Liam's voice boomed through the house as he read Fairfax his rights.

And then pandemonium.

More cops arrived and stormed through the door. She sat down on the sofa and indicated for Ralph to sit beside her. An unmistakable odor clung to him, but she was too tired and grateful to care. A stretcher was pushed through the door and Carlton was strapped onto it. Bryce loomed over his father, his face stricken. "Why did you have to kill her?"

Carlton didn't even pretend to not understand. He reached out a hand. "I did it for you, son."

Bryce ignored his father's outstretched hand and took a step back, signaling for the EMT workers to wheel him away.

"I did it for you," Carlton again insisted as he was pushed out the door.

Liam knelt in front of her, taking her hands in his. "Did he hurt you?"

"No."

He eyed her skeptically. "The side of your face is swollen. He hit you."

The outrage in his voice touched her. "It's okay." She squeezed his hands reassuringly. "If you need to go make reports, I understand."

"No way. That can wait." He cocked his head to the side, indicating the unlikely hero seated beside her. "How did this guy come to be here?"

Bryce shut the front door and returned. "Got two officers escorting my dad to the hospital. If you'd like, I can take this person down to the station and question him," he offered. "While you stay with Harper and get her statement."

"I want to hear more from him first," Liam insisted.

Actually, so did she.

Bryce positioned himself at the door and waited.

"My name's Ralph Poundstone." He gave them a wobbly smile, exposing a set of brown, crooked teeth. "Although people around here better know me as the shadow dweller. This has been my home off and on for a couple decades." He shot her an apologetic nod.

Her head reeled, her mind not fully wrapping around his bombshell news. "You've been living... here? In this house?"

"I'll show you." Ralph arose, and she and Liam followed him upstairs and then down the hallway past her bedroom. At the last guest bedroom on the right, Ralph unerringly headed to the closet and then pointed up for them to look.

A tiny crawl space in the ceiling was open, the small panel that normally covered it pushed aside.

"I never even knew this was here," she said wonderingly.

"Leads to the attic," Ralph offered helpfully. "Take a look for yourself."

He pulled a small bench in the closet directly under the opening and crawled through.

"You don't have to go up there," Liam said. "Why don't you wait for me downstairs with Bryce?"

"And miss this?" She gaped at him and shook her head. "I want to know everything. I *need* to see what's been happening right under my own nose. It will help me come to terms with my past."

Liam went in first, then reached a hand down and helped her as she wiggled through the narrow opening.

Her eyes watered at the smell as she scanned the tiny four-feet-by-six-feet enclosure that Ralph claimed as home. It was a walled-off portion of the attic. An old sleeping bag lay on the rough wood planking, surrounded by empty candy wrappers and litter. She recognized the mason jars of her mom's canned produce and preserves, and a pile of her father's old clothes. A few of her old books from middle school lay spread open on the floor.

"Why?" she asked him, shaking her head in bewilderment. "Why here?"

"It beats staying in the cold and the rain. Come spring and summer, I'd take my leave and ride the rails. Once the cold hit, I'd come back home."

He called her home his own? She shuddered and rubbed her arms. "We never saw you."

"I'd wait until you were all out of the house and then I'd slip back in. Easy to pop the lock on that back door. You should really get that fixed."

Hysterical laughter welled in her chest. The missing food, the unexplained noises, the smell, the sixth sense that screamed she wasn't alone in the house. And of course, that night he'd hovered over Presley. She should be furious, angry at the violation. While all that was true, it was also true that a weight had floated off her shoulders. She wasn't crazy.

"Why us? Why our house?" she asked.

"I was coming into town one day and happened to see your family getting in a car and going out. I was tired, cold and hungry. It occurred to me to check the doors and windows. Lucky for me, the back door was easy to pick. I came in and ate. Everything was all warm and cozy-like. So, I thinks to myself, *why not stay?* I looked around and found this hidey-hole. Hadn't planned on staying long but discovered I kinda liked it."

"Trespassing and theft." Liam quirked a brow at her. "We'll go on and take him into custody."

But she needed to know more. "Were you in the kitchen that night?"

"Presley." His hollowed-out eyes sank in deeper. "She was a good girl. She fed me several times over the years. Even brought me a blanket once."

Harper's looked at him in horrified disbelief. "She knew about you?"

"No. Not that I lived in your house. We met a few nights when I'd gone out for a bit of fresh air. She saw me shivering and brought me food and drink. I slept in your utility shed some that winter." He gestured at the tiny space. "Sometimes I felt closed in and needed a break. Anyway, that winter, I'd hear her sneak out at night. I saw who she was meeting, too. And then that night her boyfriend snuck in, I went downstairs to check on her. Heard them whispering in the basement, making plans. Then when her boyfriend left, that other man snuck in. The one that tried to kill you today."

"Carlton Fairfax. Go on."

"I seen him hit her in the back of the head and she was out cold. He carried her to the kitchen, all limp in his arms. Already dead, I think. He set her body on the floor and started fiddling around by the stove. He suddenly hightailed it out of the house, and then came the explosion. I didn't know what he was doing," Ralph assured her quickly. "It all happened so fast. When I saw the flames, I went straight to her. But it was too late. She was already gone."

None of them spoke, and in the silence, Harper sent up a little prayer to her sister. *We found him, sis. The man who murdered you. I'll make sure he's punished.*

"So that explains what you saw that night," Liam said. "Being a firefighter, Fairfax knew how to make a small, untraceable explosive. Figured there had to be a logical explanation."

"It was you who planted the jacks on the stairs

and in my bed," she said in a flash of understanding. "And it was you who sent me the messages to get out of the house. Not Kimber."

"I picked up a thing or two when riding the rails. Even got me an email account. So I used it to reach out to you. I tried to warn you. To scare you off. I was afraid he'd come back one day and hurt you, too. But you wouldn't listen."

"You'll have to find another place to live now," Liam said. "You can't stay here anymore."

She completely agreed, even while pitying Ralph. "But where will he go?"

"For now, he'll go with Bryce and make a statement. We'll keep him a few days in jail on trespassing charges until we can find a shelter with an opening."

Ralph nodded, and tears ran down his dirty cheeks. "Can I bring something with me?"

"Depends on what it is."

Ralph picked up a tattered copy of *Charlotte's Web* and held it up for her permission.

"Of course, take it," she urged.

Her emotions were all over the place as she and Liam watched Bryce take Ralph into custody.

"That odor. Think your shadow dweller has bathed any the past year? Going to be a long ride for Bryce."

She laughed, the relief from escaping her ordeal draining away. "I should have offered him use of my shower and a pair of Dad's old pants and shirt."

"Nah, Bryce deserves it after all the hard times

he's given me these last few months. Once Ralph gets to the detention center, they'll make sure he's thoroughly washed before issuing him a uniform."

"I still can't get over that he's been living with us all these years and we didn't even know it." She shivered and rubbed her arms. "So creepy. Even though he's turned out to be harmless."

Liam's face grew serious. "You've been through the wringer today. Sure you're okay?"

"Yes," she answered, surprised at the truth. "I feel relieved now that I know what happened to Presley and that her killer's been discovered."

She buried her head against Liam's chest. "Fairfax knocked her out and then started the fire. Can you imagine anything so horrible? And he had no remorse. None."

Warm fingers caressed her scalp, and she closed her eyes, concentrating on nothing but the comforting feel of his touch. Liam kissed her forehead, and she raised her eyes, finding love and concern written in his darkened eyes.

"When I knew Carlton was at your house…" His voice grew gruff, and he swallowed hard. "I've never been so scared in my life."

And this was a man who'd been shot at and faced danger every day. "I'm okay," she murmured, bestowing feather kisses along his jaw. This time, she was the one offering him comfort.

"I don't want another day to go by without telling you something I should have said almost from the very start. I love you, Harper."

She couldn't imagine a better ending to this strange, stressful day. His declaration of love helped counter Carlton's murderous revelations. Much as she'd always be saddened by Presley's death, it was time she moved forward with her own life. "Liam," she whispered, wrapping her arms around his neck, "I love you, too."

Epilogue

Harper followed Kimber around her old home, marveling at the changes she'd made in the last six months. A fresh coat of paint, combined with new flooring and light fixtures, gave the old structure a fresh boost.

"It's never looked better," she told Kimber.

"Thanks to your decorating skills. I didn't have a clue about paint colors and all that other stuff you picked out for us."

"Glad to help. Besides, it's good exposure for my new design firm."

"How's business?"

"Surprisingly good," she was happy to report. "Thanks to all your contacts."

"Good. Told you so." Kimber bounded up the stairs as she spoke over her shoulder. "Everything's on schedule for the tourist season starting next month. We're booked solid for weeks. And wait until you see what Richard and I have done with the attic."

Her old friend was beaming, like she hadn't in years. Harper obligingly entered the attic and blinked.

Drywall replaced the old brick and rough planks, and the same walnut flooring from the hallway extended here. The window had been replaced and enlarged. Sunlight poured through the room. Built-in shelves filled with books lined one wall, and a love seat and wing-back chairs were arranged in a casual sitting area.

"It's a reading room for our guests," Kimber said proudly. "A place they can privately relax in the evenings if they choose."

Curious, she stepped over to the far side where the plywood wall had been removed. Ralph's old, cramped hidey-hole was no longer. To think that for years, he'd made it his own winter home was still hard to wrap her mind around.

"Everything okay?" Kimber asked anxiously.

"Yes. Just remembering Ralph," she admitted.

Kimber shrugged dramatically. "What a creep."

"No. More a tragic figure," she gently admonished. "But he's better off where he lives now."

Ralph had been diagnosed with developmental and mental health disabilities and was eligible to reside in a halfway house, where he seemed to flourish.

"And, in the end, he was a help to you," Kimber admitted. "And to Liam's family."

The mystery of Liam's uncle Teddy had been solved. Ralph and he had been camp mates years ago at the tracks. Teddy had died of natural causes— probably pneumonia, from Ralph's description of the symptoms—and was buried in Baysville's pauper cemetery with an unmarked nameplate. Liam's mother had since erected a tombstone for her long-lost brother.

Loud footfalls ascended the stairs.

"Mommy! Someone's at the door for Miss Harper."

Surprised, Harper glanced out the window to see Liam striding up the front porch. "Wonder what he's doing here in the middle of the day?" she asked.

Kimber shrugged but looked a bit too smug. As if she was in on some private joke. "He's the new deputy police chief—reckon he can come and go as he pleases." Before Harper could question her further, Courtney, Anise and Layla appeared, chattering away in that delightful style of young girls.

Harper marched downstairs with Kimber and her girls. Her hand trailed along the familiar mahogany railing.

On the eighth step from the bottom, where Presley supposedly fell and died, she remembered her old mantra—*blessings, sis*. But it didn't fill her with sadness anymore. Like her, the old house was moving on. It felt right that it was inhabited by a family again. Hopefully, a family that would fill it with years of happy memories.

Goodbye, house, she added to her silent mantra.

At the doorway, Liam was bent on one knee, laughing at something Courtney said. Her heart flooded with joy. He'd be a wonderful father one day. Not that they'd even discussed the possibility of raising children. Yet. But they'd lived at his place since Kimber moved here. Their relationship was strong. Steady.

"What brings you here?" she asked curiously.

"Thought we could go out for a nice ride before dinner."

Funny, long drives weren't something they'd ever done before. He and Kimber exchanged a significant look. Fine, she'd find out soon enough what they were up to. So, she played along as she said goodbye to Kimber and her girls.

"Bryce know you're playing hooky?" she asked after they were underway.

"He insisted on it. Claims he can't have his top deputy working longer hours than him. Makes him look bad."

Liam smiled as he fiddled with the radio. He and Bryce had developed a close friendship after all the scandal and illegal activities they'd worked together to shut down.

And it was a gorgeous April morning, after all. Local shops had opened along the downtown strip. When they passed the large stone church at the edge of town, Harper pointed at the marquee.

"Church social this weekend to welcome the new minister," she read aloud. "That's good news."

Liam nodded his head in agreement, and they were silent a moment, thinking of Allen's victims.

Allen Spencer had been found guilty on three counts of sexual abuse and was in prison.

"How's Gunner liking the new job there at the church?" she asked.

"Loves it. Takes pride in keeping the place spotless. The congregation claims it's never been so well kept. They shower him with attention and casseroles."

The bustle of town faded, and she relaxed, enjoying the view, not paying the slightest attention to where they were going. Until Kimber's old farmhouse came into view. To her astonishment, Liam turned off the county road and headed up their driveway. She was even more surprised when he pulled out a set of house keys from his pocket.

"Let's go inside and take a look."

Even with all the furniture gone, the house's charm remained. Harper strode into the kitchen and looked around. "I know Kimber and Richard are happy to be rid of the place, but I couldn't bear to sell it if it were mine."

Liam's arm wrapped around her waist from behind. "What do you say we buy it, then?"

"What?" She laughed and turned around to face him. "You're joking, right?"

"Perfectly serious. I know how much you love this place."

"But…" Her voice trailed off as she thought of all the reasons it wouldn't be a good idea.

Liam bent on one knee and took her hands in his. Seemed today was full of surprises.

"Marry me, Harper."

All her objections flew out the window. Together, they could work out the details. "Is that a question or a demand?" she teased.

Liam winked and tugged her down beside him on the kitchen floor. "Whatever you want it to be."

Much, much later, Liam surprised her yet again when he pulled out a bottle of champagne and a cake from the fridge.

"You were mighty sure of my answer, weren't you?" she said with a laugh.

This time, instead of laughing, he pulled her body up against his own in a tight embrace. "I'd never take you for granted like that. Now are you going to marry me or what?"

"You just try to slip away," she whispered, practically bursting with happiness. "And the answer is a big ole *hell yeah*."

* * * * *

If you enjoyed Unmasking the Shadow Man
by Debbie Herbert,
don't miss Warning Shot *by Jenna Kernan,*
available November 2019 wherever
Harlequin Intrigue books and ebooks are sold.

Get 4 FREE REWARDS!

We'll send you 2 FREE Books plus 2 FREE Mystery Gifts.

Harlequin Intrigue® books feature heroes and heroines that confront and survive danger while finding themselves irresistibly drawn to one another.

FREE
Value Over
$20

"Let's try this again." Logan wiped his dusty palm against his
shirt and held out his hand. "I'm Captain Logan Hess with US
Delta Force."

Her mouth formed an O but at least she took his hand this time
in a firm grip, her skin rough against his. "I'm Lana Moreno, but
you probably already know that, don't you?"

"I sure do." He jerked his thumb over his shoulder. "I saw
your little impromptu news conference about an hour ago."

"But you knew who I was before that. You didn't track me
down to compare cowboy boots." She jabbed him in the chest
with her finger. "Did you know Gilbert?"

"Unfortunately, no." Lana didn't need to know just how
unfortunate that really was. "Let's get out of the dirt and grab
some lunch."

She tilted her head and a swathe of dark hair fell over her
shoulder, covering one eye. The other eye scorched his face.
"Why should I have lunch with you? What do you want from

me? When I heard you were Delta Force, I thought you might have known Gilbert, might've known what happened at that outpost."

"I didn't, but I know of Gilbert and the rest of them, even the assistant ambassador who was at the outpost. I can guarantee I know a lot more about the entire situation than you do from reading that redacted report they grudgingly shared with you."

"You are up-to-date. What are we waiting for?" Her feet scrambled beneath her as she slid up the wall. "If you have any information about the attack in Nigeria, I want to hear it."

"I thought you might." He rose from the ground, towering over her petite frame. He pulled a handkerchief from the inside pocket of his leather jacket and waved it at her. "Take this."

"Thank you." She blew her nose and mopped her face, running a corner of the cloth beneath each eye to clean up her makeup. "I suppose you don't want it back."

"You can wash it for me and return it the next time we meet."

That statement earned him a hard glance from those dark eyes, still sparkling with unshed tears, but he had every intention of seeing Lana Moreno again and again—however many times it took to pick her brain about why she believed there was more to the story than a bunch of Nigerian criminals deciding to attack an embassy outpost. It was a ridiculous cover story if he ever heard one.

About as ridiculous as the story of Major Rex Denver working with terrorists.

Her quest had to be motivated by more than grief over a brother. People didn't stage stunts like she just did in front of a congressman's office based on nothing.

Don't miss
Enemy Infiltration *by Carol Ericson,*
available November 2019 wherever
Harlequin® Intrigue books and ebooks are sold.

www.Harlequin.com

Looking for more satisfying love stories
with community and family at their core?

Check out **Harlequin® Special Edition**
and **Love Inspired®** books!

New books available every month!

CONNECT WITH US AT:

Facebook.com/groups/HarlequinConnection

 Facebook.com/HarlequinBooks

Twitter.com/HarlequinBooks

 Instagram.com/HarlequinBooks

Pinterest.com/HarlequinBooks

ReaderService.com

**ROMANCE WHEN
YOU NEED IT**